BEETLE BUNKER

ZONDERKIDZ

Beetle Bunker

This is a work of fiction. The characters, incidents, and dialogue are products of the author's imagination and are not to be construed as real. Any resemblance to actual events or persons, living or dead, is entirely coincidental.

Requests for information should be addressed to:

Zonderkidz, 5300 Patterson Ave. SE, Grand Rapids, Michigan 49530

Library of Congress Cataloging-in-Publication Data

Elmer, Robert.
Beetle bunker / by Robert Elmer.
p. cm.—(The wall series ; bk. 2)
Summary: In 1961, thirteen-year-old Sabine, an adventurer despite being crippled by polio, finds a forgotten bunker which might allow her, her family, and friends to reach freedom by tunneling under the Berlin Wall, or might lead to far greater danger.
ISBN-13: 978-0-310-70944-2 (softcover)
1. Berlin (Germany—History—1945-1990—Juvenile fiction. [1. Berlin (Germany)—History—1945-1990—Fiction. 2. Berlin Wall, Berlin, Germany, 1961-1989—Fiction. 3. Family life—Germany—Fiction. 4. People with disabilities—Fiction. 5. Christian life—Fiction. 6. Germany—History—1945–1990—Fiction.] I. Title. II. Series: Elmer, Robert. Wall series ; bk. 2.
PZ7.E4794Bde 2006
[Fic]—dc22

2006001931

Published in association with the literary agency of Alive Communications, Inc., 7680 Goddard St., Ste. 200, Colorado Springs, Colorado 80920.

Editor: Kristen Tuinstra
Art direction: Merit Alderink
Cover design: Jay Smith of Juicebox Design
Interior design: Ruth Bandstra
Interior composition: Ruth Bandstra

Printed in the United States of America

BEETLE BUNKER

BY ROBERT ELMER

ZONDERVAN.com/
AUTHORTRACKER
follow your favorite authors

CONTENTS

PROLOGUE

ST. LUDWIG'S HOSPITAL, EAST BERLIN

APRIL 1955

"We will wait until you decide to stop blubbering, Sabine Becker. Until then, you can just stay in there."

Seven-year-old Sabine sat on the closet floor and shivered, holding her head in her hands.

Tomboys never cry, she told herself. But no matter what, she could not stop the sobs.

"B-b-b-bitte," she repeated, over and over. "P-p-p-please. I d-d-don't want to d-d-do any more today.... It hurts s-s-so much—"

But begging had never worked with Nurse Ilse. Neither had deal-making or screams or tantrums or hunger strikes. Even smiles and promises to do better later only brought a slap on the hand from the ruler Nurse Ilse carried in her apron pocket.

"We can wait as long as you like," said the nurse, "but we *will* return to your exercises." She turned the key in the lock and walked away. As her footsteps grew fainter, Sabine closed her eyes.

She didn't let herself fall asleep, though. What if Mama came while she was asleep? Nurse Ilse wouldn't wake her. She only did that in the middle of the night, when she pinched

Sabine's cheek to get her attention, then forced nasty medicine down her throat. It was supposed to make her polio better.

Sabine bumped her head against the inside of the door and shivered. She prayed to her mother's Jesus and talked to her own made-up friends—like the characters from the books Mama read to her. Sometimes she wasn't sure which was which, though she would never dare admit that to Mama.

At least for a little while she was away from Nurse Ilse. Here she could escape to her pretend world, the place where she could walk and run, just like all the other kids.

Only not forever. Nurse Ilse came back a few minutes later with another threat, this one worse than locking her in a closet.

"If you continue to raise such a fuss, your mother will never be able to visit again. Never. Do you hear me?"

"I don't believe you," Sabine answered defiantly.

Maybe next time Mama will finally take me home again, Sabine thought.

Rheinsbergerstrasse. Home. To Oma's crowded apartment on Rheinsberger Street in East Berlin. Where she'd lived all her life with her mama and her ancient grandmother, Oma Poldi Becker, and her half brother, Erich. He was twenty years old and wanted to be a doctor. She tried to remember his stories about hiding on an American airplane with his cousin Katarina when he was thirteen. He even said they flew to an American air base with Sabine's father, who had been an Air Force sergeant. Sabine wasn't sure she believed it all, but of course it made her jealous of Erich. He had known her American father, while all she had were stories about his sense of humor—and about the plane crash.

If I could go home today, she decided, *I'd never complain about Onkel Heinz and Tante Gertrud again.* Her uncle and aunt had moved into Oma's apartment a couple of years ago. It made things a little crowded, but Uncle Heinz had shown her how to tell the difference between a Mercedes and a Volkswagen. She knew she wasn't supposed to care, because she was a girl, but she did anyway. He could get bossy sometimes, though, and he belched a lot. Especially when he drank beer.

Even Aunt Gertrud's ranting and smoking wouldn't seem too bad, if only—

"Out, now!" growled Nurse Ilse, startling Sabine as she unlocked the door. "You have a visitor."

Sabine blinked at the bright lights but smiled as the nurse carried her back to bed. Wait until she could show Mama—

Her mother stood in the doorway of the hospital room only a few minutes later, her mouth and nose hidden behind a blue hospital mask but her eyes twinkling with tears. She had to wear the mask and a hospital gown just like everybody else, so she wouldn't catch Sabine's polio.

"Sabine!" Mama held out her arms as if to hug her only daughter, which of course she could not.

"I've been waiting for you all week, Mama." Sabine couldn't help grinning from ear to ear. Maybe polio could turn her legs to limp noodles, but it could not keep Mama from her weekly visit. Sabine knew that more than anything. And now it was time for the surprise she and Jesus had been working on for days, in secret, when nobody was looking.

Watch this, Nurse Ilse! Sabine grabbed the corner of her sheet, and a moment later she rolled her left shoulder so her weight would carry her off the edge of the bed.

"No! What do you think you're doing?" Nurse Ilse fumed as she dropped her clipboard. But Sabine would swing her legs around and show them she wasn't disabled any longer. See? Just as she'd hoped, her bare feet cleared the edge of her bed and hit the cold, slick tile of the hospital floor.

Now, Jesus! she prayed silently. *Please, now! Make my legs strong!*

Only maybe she should have prayed out loud. She later decided that must have been what she did wrong. What else could it have been? Not enough faith, she decided. She should have said something out loud, the way Jesus did, like, "Rise, take up thy pallet and walk!" Only Sabine wasn't sure what a pallet was.

And as both her mother and the nurse lunged for her, Sabine's knees wiggled for a moment. Then they buckled and sent her sprawling face-first to the scrubbed tile floor.

She remembered how the yucky smell of floor cleaner made her throat burn and her stomach turn. But she remembered nothing else. When she woke up, she found herself tucked tightly once again into her bed, her prison of sheets. How long had it been? Two minutes? Ten? Her cheekbones throbbed with pain as if someone had slapped her. She knew that feeling. But she did not open her eyes, only lay still and listened to the two women arguing in the hallway.

"You don't seem to understand how serious this is, Frau Becker. If you don't leave now, I'm going to have to call security."

"But that's my *daughter* in there."

"Your daughter will be fine, no thanks to you. Now—"

"Wait a minute. How was this my fault?"

"If you continue to fill her head with religious nonsense, I'll have no choice but to file a report. You see what it's done today. She actually seems to believe what you tell her about"—she spit out the words—"this *God* healing her legs."

Sabine didn't hear her mother's response. But she was ready to throw her bedpan at the evil nurse. Nurse Ilse went on, threatening to find a more suitable home for Sabine after her hospital treatment—if the "religious nonsense" didn't stop.

And even polio could not stop Sabine's tears.

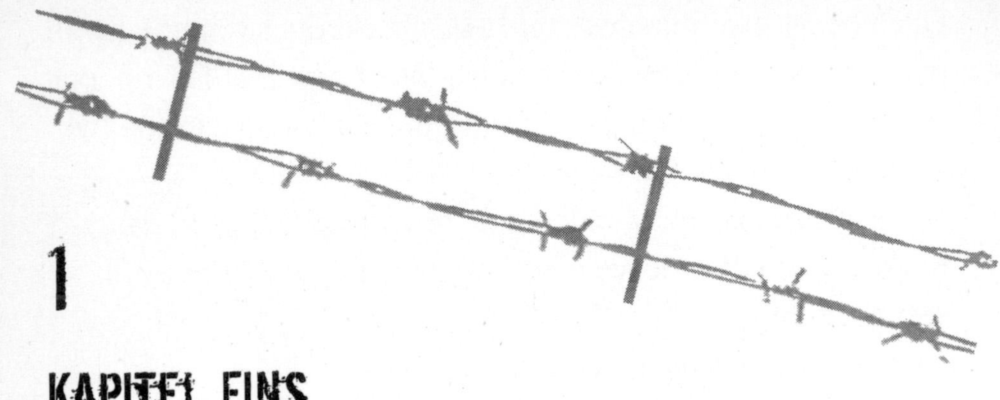

1

KAPITEL EINS

BERLIN, GERMANY

MAY 1961: SIX YEARS LATER...

"Not again!"

Sabine groaned when she rounded the corner, adjusting the crutch clamps around her wrists and arms. Up ahead, it looked like construction workers had begun tearing up Brunnenstrasse once more. Maybe this time they wouldn't stare at her as she limped by on her walking crutches, more like canes that strapped to her forearms. In the past six years, since getting out of the hospital, Sabine had heard all the cruel jokes. So what? She could walk okay, now, even with the brace on her right leg that no one saw. And she couldn't stay home the rest of her life, just like she couldn't stay in the hospital. This was 1961, after all.

So she gripped the handles of her crutches a little more tightly, took a deep breath, and stared straight ahead. She would ignore them, just as she always tried to ignore the neighborhood spy, Wolfgang. Did you get a package from the West? Comrade Wolfgang would want to know. A visitor? Wolfgang would report it to the government. Out too late? Wolfgang was always watching. And the people he watched usually received a visit from the *Vopo* security police, or worse.

Ja, compared to Wolfgang, these construction guys seemed pretty tame. Or she hoped they were. But no spy and no construction workers would keep her from visiting her brother, Erich, at the hospital where he worked. If she had to circle around the block on Bergstrasse, that would probably add half an hour to her walk. Not this time.

To the right, a large older apartment building cast a ragged shadow across the street. The top two stories had collapsed in an American bombing raid during the war, leaving crumbled piles of stone and rusting, twisted steel. That had happened years before Sabine was born, but things didn't change very quickly in East Berlin. Not like in the western half of the city.

But not to worry. It looked like the construction crew up ahead had taken a break. One of the men sat in the back of his truck, hands clasped behind his neck, eyes closed in a midday nap. The early summer sunshine hit him in the face. Fine. The others had left their pile of water pipes on the sidewalk, blocking the way with a sign that read "CAUTION! NO ENTRY!" in big block letters. But who knew when they would return? Everyone seemed to have cleared out for lunch. A typical hard-working Tuesday in the Soviet sector of East Berlin.

Limping past the warning sign, Sabine glanced down. Flimsy boards covered part of a gaping hole in the sidewalk. An unsteady ladder slanted down about ten feet to an exposed pipe. From top to bottom, they'd laid a canvas tarp out like a slide.

Careful, she cautioned herself as she stepped past the sign. Without warning, a board gave way, launching her right over the edge. Sabine could hardly yelp as she fell; the best she could do was to plant her crutches on the tarp, like a skier sliding down an alpine slope.

But a good deal less graceful. She lost her balance and slid down the slope on the seat of her pants, crutches waving like windmills. The tarp pulled loose, and an avalanche of dirt followed her down, down, down—she slammed into a crumbling brick foundation wall, crutches first. Ouch.

"Ack!" Sabine coughed and struggled to breathe. She'd bent the tip of one crutch, but it was still usable. The brace on her leg had loosened up a bit, but no problem there, either. Had she broken anything? Her arms moved all right, though she'd twisted her right elbow a bit during the tumble. If that was all she'd injured, she'd been spared.

Thank you. She breathed out the words in a quick prayer and struggled to rise. Had Wolfgang seen her fall? She hoped not. No telling what the workers would do to her if they found her down here. How soon would Erich come looking? He knew the route she would take, but he might just think she'd forgotten about visiting. And he might be too busy to worry about her.

A couple more loose bricks fell with a *thunk.*

She clutched her head for a moment, trying to decide what to do. She couldn't climb up the rickety ladder without help. And for certain she didn't want to meet up with any angry construction workers—not after she'd ignored their warning signs. Maybe she should just see what she'd stumbled onto.

And *ja,* she could just imagine what her mother would say about *that*! "Sabine Becker, I thought little girls were supposed to play with dolls, not—"

Not explore old ruined buildings? Well, that's what famous explorers did. So why not her? And why not here in Berlin? She couldn't discover ancient civilizations, but this might be the next best thing. She used her crutch to knock away a couple more bricks, then... there! Look at that! She peered into the little cave she found that had just opened up at the bottom of the workers' dig. More like a basement, actually. Through the dog-sized opening she could make out the dim outline of cement walls and floors, maybe connected to the old apartment building upstairs. She knew that no one had lived in this bombed-out building for years.

She whispered a shy "Guten Tag?" into the darkness and waited for the echo of her hello to return. And she shivered at the draft of stale, musty air that hit her in the face. *Hmm. Is this what it's like to discover a pharaoh's tomb?*

Faint slivers of sunlight streamed down from above, filtered through cracks in the upper floors. Maybe she could find another way out, up through the ruined building's basement. That way she could escape before anyone found her. *Okay,* she thought. *Here goes.*

2

KAPITEL ZWEI

THE BUNKER

For the first few minutes, Sabine felt her way like a blind girl with a cane, taking care not to place her crutches in holes in the floor or cracks in the cement. And as her eyes slowly adjusted to the cellar, she began to realize what this place was, really.

"A bunker," she whispered to herself. A bomb shelter. Deep cellar. Storage room. Definitely much more than your everyday basement. The ceiling had collapsed here and there, leaving piles of charred timbers like twisted toothpicks. That had opened it up just enough to let in filtered light here and there, through the floor of the ruined building upstairs. But what was all this stuff?

In the first room, she ran her finger along the top of a metal drum, stacked against a wall with a dozen more. It smelled faintly of fuel, maybe gasoline, though when she hit a drum with the end of her crutch, it rang empty.

"Doesn't look like anyone's been down here since the war." Her quiet words echoed in the cavelike main room and the others that opened into it. Each was separated by a heavy-duty metal door, almost big enough for a streetcar to drive through. When she pushed on one, it gave way with a loud complaint of rusty metal hinges.

Wow. She picked her way slowly through other shadowy rooms, each one more interesting than the last. In the next room, someone had piled wooden crates full of rusty metal cans clear up to the ceiling. Sabine picked up a can that had been punctured in the bombing raids and held it high to catch a faint ray of sunshine.

Trinkwasser. The emergency drinking water had long ago gone dry. She wondered what it might have tasted like, though, or even if it would still be any good after all these years. But there were more rooms to explore.

In room number three she could make out a small radio receiver on the floor; it had slipped off an overturned table at some point and looked pretty beat up. Sabine tried all the switches. Nothing.

She found the biggest surprise in the last room. She smelled the stale air and sneezed. More stinky fuel? Not exactly. She peered at the shell of a small car, perched on cement blocks, collecting a thick layer of dust.

"Well, there's not much left of it," she told no one in particular, "but it looks like an old Volkswagen."

Uncle Heinz would have been excited to see this. From the looks of it, this had to be a World War 2 Beetle, the kind with a convertible top that folded down. Sort of like the Volkswagen sedan she saw on the streets over in the West, in the American and French sectors of the city. This one was missing the back seat, but it still had the two front seats, a steering wheel, an engine in the back (mostly in pieces), and a windshield (totally cracked). All four of the wheels were missing, though. Well, what did she expect? But the big question was—

"How did they ever get this thing down here?"

She looked around for a big enough opening, but the far wall had crumbled; it ended in a pile of dirt and concrete chunks. Had this been an underground parking garage, as well as a bomb shelter? Maybe. She slipped into the driver's seat and spun the wheel. Ha! Wouldn't Erich love this too—driving a twenty-year-old army staff car around Berlin—

But no. Only a few people she knew of owned cars in the Soviet sector. And they only drove noisy, smelly little cars called Trabants—Trabis—made in East Germany. She sighed and bounced on the seat a little. A spring started to pop through.

Oh, well. Maybe she would come back to this place. With a couple of candles and a nice blanket to cover the rotten seats, it could make a perfect reading retreat. A place to get away. If she could just find a way to get in and out of the bunker.

Hmm. That could be a problem. But as she poked around the other rooms a bit more, she wondered why she couldn't find a ladder. "Or," she mused as she checked a dark corner, "a stairway!"

There! She looked up at a circular staircase and tested the first step with her crutch. It protested loudly. Okay. Shifting both crutches to her left hand, she did her best to hold her weight up by gripping the railing and taking each step slowly. Up to the second step, then the third—

Minutes later, she pushed up at the boards that covered the only other way out.

"Come on!" she grunted, using the ends of her crutches as hammers to loosen the trapdoor. "Open up!"

Not very ladylike, perhaps, but it worked. After a couple more hits, one of the boards gave a little, even splintering in the corner. She could peek out through the crack into the ground floor of the ruined, empty apartment building above her. She saw a bit of peeling rose wallpaper. Now she knew where she was, sort of. And what to look for. She gave the board another jab for good measure, forgetting where the edge of the steps—

"Au!" All she could do was hang on to the railing as she slid halfway down, fireman-style. Her feet followed behind, hitting every step hard. She eased herself all the way to the floor. Well, she came down a little faster than she went up, didn't she? In the process, she'd lost a crutch, which had clattered down to the cement floor before her.

Which probably wasn't a bad thing. By the time she had recovered her lost crutch, she heard a voice echoing through the bunker.

"Suh-BEEE-nuh!" Even from a distance, she could make out Erich's call. "Sabine! Are you down here?"

"Erich!" she answered back. She squinted as she limped through the bunker and neared the hole in the foundation. "I'm right here!"

"I see that." Erich still wore his white hospital smock as he peeked inside. "The question is, what in the world are you *doing* down a hole like this? *Bist du verrückt?*"

"*Nein*, I'm not crazy!"

By that time, several construction workers had joined Erich at the top of the hole to see what was going on. Sabine looked down at herself as she thought of how to explain. Good thing she'd been wearing her brother's hand-me-down pants, the ones her mother never let her wear to church. A dress in this situation would have been a disaster.

"But," she finally added, planting a hand on her hip, "I could sure use a hand out of this hole, please."

Which came swiftly as Erich hurried down the ladder and helped her back up, one step at a time.

"I started to get worried when you didn't meet me at the hospital at noon," he told her. "You weren't back at the apartment, either. Then when I ran by this hole, I saw workers looking down. They said they'd heard a noise. Like something collapsed. That was you?"

"Probably sewer rats," she told him. "I had to fight off a few."

Erich just harrumphed; he knew when Sabine was kidding. And Sabine knew Erich had probably been running up and down the streets, searching for her. The athletic twenty-six-year-old hospital intern was always like that. Erich the Rescuer. Erich, always protecting her. She felt like a rag doll as he lifted her back to the street while the workers gathered around to stare.

"Quite a discovery, eh, boys?" Erich said as Sabine held her crutches out to either side like wings. "A perfectly preserved Egyptian mummy. Living down in the sewer for ten thousand years. She can even still talk!"

A couple of the men chuckled as she dusted herself off and pointed to the broken board, the little platform that had dumped her into the hole. "But really, you guys ought to fix that. A person could get hurt. I mean, I was walking just fine before I fell in there. Now look at me. I need crutches."

See? She could be a comedian too. As long as her older brother was there to cover for her. She smiled at Erich before starting back toward home.

"Thanks for coming after me, though. It was kind of dusty down there. Made me sneeze."

Erich scratched his sandy hair. "So did you see anything?" His curiosity must have gotten the better of him.

"Oh, you know, the usual Nazi treasure, gold and stuff, hidden for twenty years."

Which (except for the gold part) was partly true. But Erich wasn't buying it.

"Listen, Sabine, you've really got to be more careful." He followed her, but Sabine didn't slow down. "There are holes and old bunkers and broken sewers like that all over the city. It seems like every time they start a construction project or tear down another bombed-out building, they find something strange underground. If I didn't come to find you—"

"I could have gotten out." Still she didn't slow down.

"Oh, come on. And look at yourself. What are you going to tell Mutti when you get home? That you were out playing in the sandbox? You're a mess!"

Sabine stopped and looked at herself for the first time. The knees of her brother's cast-off pants had ripped, and she was coated with dust. She knew Erich had a point, especially when she looked up at Wolfgang's window and saw him watching them through his binoculars. She scowled at him but couldn't help feeling like a bug under a microscope. And yes, he would likely take notes and probably call the authorities. But worse than that—

Her mother would not be pleased.

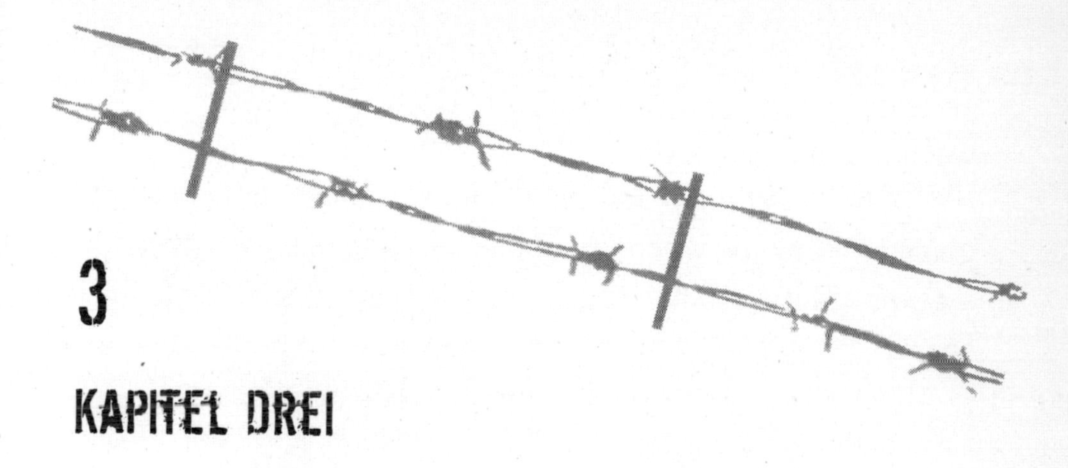

3

KAPITEL DREI

ESCAPING THE GOATEE

"Sabine, stop reading that stupid storybook and pay attention to the broadcast!" Uncle Heinz's words startled her, but he'd barely opened his eyes as he reclined. Oma Poldi's old flowered couch sagged under his weight. Sabine wasn't quite sure how he managed to fit on it. But he had claimed it for his own, and she rarely saw him anywhere else.

Aunt Gertrud moaned from her chair in the corner, black shades covering her eyes and a smoldering cigarette dangling from her lips. So maybe it didn't look like a good East German socialist worker thing to wear. But she said she could "see" her migraines even with the blinders on.

"Bitte, Onkel Heinz... please." Sabine knew it would do no good. She could count on only three people in this world—and he was not one of them. But Oma was confined to her bed, as usual, while Sabine's mother and brother were still at work.

Her uncle belched like a bullfrog (no "excuse me," or anything) and wagged a pudgy finger at her the way he did when no one was around to defend her.

"Don't Onkel Heinz me. I'm doing you a favor. In fact, you're going to thank me when you go back to school tomorrow and you can tell the teacher what Comrade Ulbricht said in his speech. Every good young Communist needs to know this."

"I'm not a good young Communist." She lifted her book even higher to cover her face. "I'm a Christian, and I don't like the Goatee."

The Goatee was their nickname for Walter Ulbricht, the leader of Communist East Germany, and it was all his fault. The man trimmed his beard like that; what did he expect? The way Sabine saw it, he deserved every nickname they could give him.

"Have a little respect, eh?" Uncle Heinz puffed his cheeks. "One of these days, I'm not going to be able to help you anymore. You and your mother both. If she weren't my sister—"

She'd heard that line before. Next he would remind her, again, of her duties to the state, what faithful Communist working masses were supposed to do every day. Just like the big red banners that draped East Berlin's drab buildings said: Work hard. Stay away from spy-infested West Berlin. Support the people's factories and the German Democratic Republic. Meet your work quotas. Never mind that Uncle Heinz, the good Communist, spent most of his time right here on the couch. He wasn't even really related to Oma, his sister's mother-in-law.

But he and Aunt Gertrud had invited themselves for a visit to Oma's apartment and had never left.

Sabine kept reading *Black Beauty*, a horse story she'd especially liked the first two times she'd read it. And she did her best to block out the put-me-to-sleep drone of Comrade Ulbricht's speech, broadcast on the official East German state radio station. Suddenly the novel flew from her hands.

"What did your onkel tell you?" Aunt Gertrud glared down her long nose at Sabine; she'd pulled back the sleep mask and had parked it on her forehead. Sabine thought all she needed was a wart and a black hat to complete the look. And maybe a broomstick.

Black Beauty lay on the floor, facedown. Sabine sighed and stooped to pick it up. Aunt Gertrud would never dare act like this when Sabine's mother was around.

"But we've heard it all, Tante Gertrud. He goes on and on about how terrible the capitalists in the West are—the decadent Americans and their puppets, the West Berliners."

"Well, of course they are."

Oh, dear. Sabine wasn't going to try to understand what the screaming men were saying. Comrade Ulbricht and his friends just repeated what the Russians told them to say. She believed that the only puppets were right there in East Berlin.

"He says much more than that," Uncle Heinz told them, lifting a finger to his lips. "You just have to listen."

"Can't I change it to the station that plays Frank Sinatra songs?" Sabine wondered aloud. Aunt Gertrud glared once more and settled back into her chair, pulling the sleep mask back over her eyes. Sabine pretended to listen while waiting for her chance to run. Her mother wouldn't be home for another two hours.

At least it wasn't hard to tell when Uncle Heinz fell asleep again. His hands twitched once, and his lips and cheeks puffed out like a blowfish. On the radio, Comrade Ulbricht was just getting warmed up.

"The enemy is trying to use the open border between the German Democratic Republic and West Berlin to undermine our government and its economy—," he droned on. "Aggressive forces and subversive centers—" blah-blah. "Serious losses in our workforce—" more blah-blah.

And Aunt Gertrud's mask still covered her eyes. Sabine took the chance to quietly limp to the dining room table and grab her book.

If she was extra careful, maybe—

In the kitchen, she found a couple of candle stubs and some matches, which she slipped into her little backpack. She also grabbed a couple of scraps of bread as she quietly made her way to the door.

"You're not leaving, are you, child?" Aunt Gertrud screeched. "You know how upset your mother was last time, with all that dirt and—"

"Be back in just a few minutes, Tante Gertrud." Sabine didn't slow down to explain, didn't wait for the door to close behind her as she hustled down the hall and down the outside steps, into the late afternoon sunshine. Never mind that Wolfgang would probably see her. She glanced up at his third-floor window and sighed with relief. Empty.

"Sabine!" Aunt Gertrud's screech followed her outside. Sabine bit her lip.

"You should listen to your tante." The quiet, menacing voice made her jump. Wolfgang, his arms crossed in challenge, stepped out of a doorway to block her way. "A person like you could get hurt."

As if he cared. Comrade Wolfgang would be pleased only when they came to take Sabine and her family away, as "Enemies of the State."

"Danke for your concern," she said, trying not to let the fear creep into her voice. But as she passed the gangly man with the wrinkled shirt and tousled black hair, she could smell the darkness on his breath. Or was it just that he hadn't taken a bath in weeks?

"Sabine!" Aunt Gertrud's voice faded behind her as Sabine grabbed a stair railing for balance, then hobbled toward the ruined apartment building on Bergstrasse as fast as her noodle legs would carry her. Someday, she told herself, she'd run without her dumb crutches. For now, she worried that Wolfgang might follow her.

But he didn't—this time. And as she passed Number 14, she heard the familiar woof of the dog that no one claimed. He bounded out of an alleyway.

"Hey, Bismarck!" She smiled with relief and bent down to scratch his ear. She didn't mind that he had been named after a famous war hero, or that he sometimes tried to run off with her crutches. "Sorry I don't have anything for you this time."

But the German shepherd mutt had already sniffed out her backpack and knew better. He parked himself on the sidewalk, right in front of Sabine, and sat up on his hind legs.

"You little beggar." Sabine dug into her backpack for the treat, a small crumble of dried cheese. "You can't follow me around the whole neighborhood."

But unlike Wolfgang, he did, all the way down Bernauer-strasse and past the tall steeple of the once-beautiful *Versöhnungskirche,* the Reconciliation Church on Ackerstrasse. Finally they came to the bombed-out apartment block, where Sabine hoped to find the entrance to the bunker. Wolfgang would have lost interest in her by now, wouldn't he?

"It's hidden in the floor," Sabine explained to her friend, who sniffed around the ruins. Come to think of it, the dog might be good to have around. Just in case.

"What do you think?" she asked Bismarck, who scampered across piles of rubble and concrete, with no problem at all. If only she could borrow his legs once in a while.

Finally she struggled into a room with peeling rose wall-paper. *This must be it.* Bomb blasts from long ago had left gaping holes in the walls and ceiling, and Sabine could see right out to the American sector. She dropped to her knees and searched the floorboards for any sign of the trapdoor—the one that blocked the circular staircase below. Bismarck helped with a few sniffs.

"Thanks, boy." She ran a hand across the rough, weather-beaten floor. "It's not as easy to find as I hoped. Maybe you can—ouch!"

Something sharp poked her finger, like a sliver. *Au!* But that was okay if it was the board she'd split the other day, pounding on the door from beneath. She followed the board and saw the splintered corner of the trapdoor. Yes!

She set to work prying it open with her crutch, pulling out the nails, lifting it up. *Whew!* She could see how the hidden trapdoor had stayed hidden for so long. Nervously, she checked over her shoulder once more. No telling if a friend of Wolfgang's had followed her here.

"Here we go!" she told her friend. Bismarck turned circles and barked as Sabine lowered herself down. The dog jumped down after her. From the top of the staircase, she held the dog's collar and waited for her eyes to adjust.

"Let me show you something." She stooped low and closed the trapdoor over their heads. "I think you're going to like it."

Bismarck didn't wait, he just bounded down the stairs she had to take one at a time. He wagged his tail at her and ran off to sniff. She whistled at him, keeping him close as she set up her reading retreat in the Volkswagen staff car. First she lit her two candles, setting them just behind the shattered windshield. They lit her area pretty well, actually, and Bismarck even jumped aboard for a ride. After circling a few times, he made himself comfy in the back of the car, while Sabine curled up on her blanket in the front.

"Not bad, huh, boy?" She pulled out her book and returned to the chapter she'd been reading when Aunt Gertrud had snapped the book away. Without a breeze, the candles barely flickered. Sabine listened to the quiet of her own breathing... and the dog's. Pretty soon she just closed her eyes.

"What's going on?" She sat up with a start. The candles had nearly burned down, but Bismarck still kept watch. "How long did I sleep?"

Bismarck nuzzled her arm and thunked his tail as if to say he was ready to get home too.

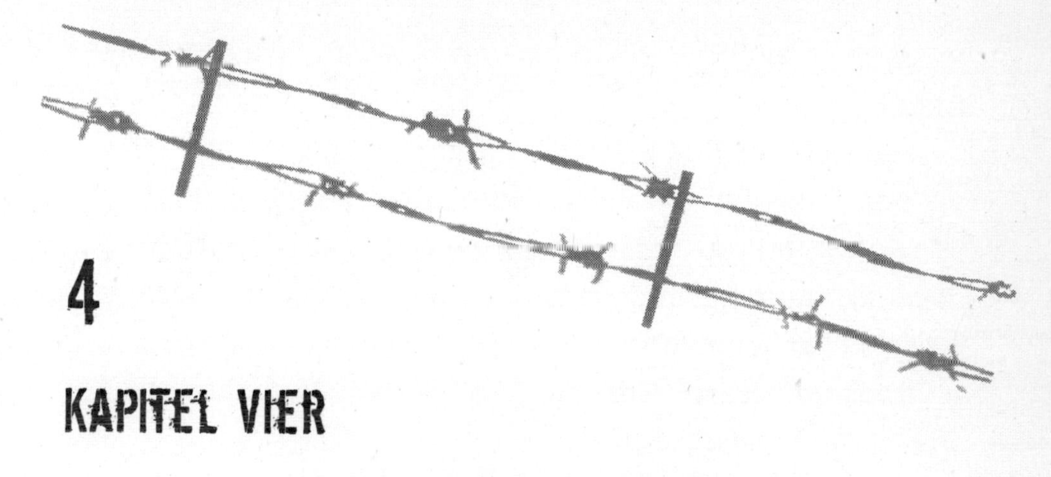

4

KAPITEL VIER

THE RIGHT THING

"Where in the world have *you* been?" Sabine's mother wiped her hands on a dish towel as her daughter slipped into a chair at the little kitchen table. The others stopped eating long enough to frown at her. And Aunt Gertrud looked over at Frau Becker to see what she would do next.

"Sorry I'm late." Sabine's mind raced to think of the right way to say it. Cabbage and potatoes looked as if they had long ago collapsed into a cold heap in the middle of her plate. "I was... I mean, I—"

Her mother's lifted eyebrows looked as if they were saying, "Yes?"

"I was reading, and I fell asleep." Sabine blurted out the truth. Maybe not the *whole* truth, but—

"Not again, Sabine." Frau Becker reached over and brushed a stray wisp of hair from Sabine's face. "And look at you. You look as if you've been... digging ditches or something."

Sabine's mother couldn't know how close she'd come to the truth.

In the silence that followed, Uncle Heinz helped himself to an extra spoonful of watered-down brown gravy.

"So why do you always sneak away to read those books of yours?" Aunt Gertrud wanted to know. "Isn't our company good enough for you?"

"Gertrud, please!" That put Sabine's mother on the defensive. "I can handle this."

"Just like you handle her staying home from school all the time? Just like you coddle her? 'Oh, my poor baby can't walk, we mustn't distress my poor baby.' "

Frau Becker's eyes filled with tears the way they had so many times before, but Gertrud wasn't done yet.

"What I don't understand is why you even stay here, if you hate East Berlin so much. Why don't you just pack your bags and run back to the West, the way all your friends are doing?"

As if they could just do that—without risking being arrested for trying.

"You can't talk to my mother like that!" Sabine stuck her chin out and would have said something else, but her mother shushed her.

"You know very well why we stay, Gertrud." Frau Becker's voice sounded as still as Gertrud's sounded shrill. "Not because we enjoy being locked up in a police state, or because we're forced to stay, which we are. But because I've already lost two husbands, and I will *not* just run away and leave her.

Even if I could. Do you understand what I'm saying? I made her that promise even before I joined—"

She stopped short, but that wasn't good enough for Gertrud.

"Go ahead and say it."

But Sabine's mother only shook her head.

"Then I will finish for you. Before you joined the Communist Party. Why don't you say so?"

Sabine held her breath. *Could it be true?* Her mother finally looked up with tears in her eyes.

"I'm not proud of it. But it was the only way to get help for Sabine. They said they would take care of her...her treatment."

"And now look how well she gets around." Gertrud swept her hand at Sabine.

"No. They gave her crutches, and that's the end of it. They broke their promise. But maybe the Americans would be no better, so I will not break mine."

Aunt Gertrud shrugged as Frau Becker went on.

"And since we're the only ones left to take care of Oma, we remain—for now. It's that simple."

Of course *Oma* meant Sabine's grandmother, who lay ill in her bed most of the time. But Aunt Gertrud would not back down. She held her forehead with both hands.

"Aw, it just gives me a headache. You and that foolish promise again. You know she can't hold you to it. And we all know she belongs in a *genesungsheim.*"

"That's enough, Gertrud." Uncle Heinz looked up from stuffing his face, but she shook him off. Sabine's mother leaned over so her nose practically touched her sister-in-law's. Aunt Gertrud didn't blink. "Let me tell you something, Gertrud, just so you don't forget." Her voice trembled this time as it rose. "As long as I live, and as long as Oma lives, she will never be put away in a rest home, out of sight. Do we understand each other? And what's more—"

A bell tinkled from Oma Poldi's room, just as someone knocked on the door. Frau Becker paused and looked toward Oma's room then toward the front door.

"Go see what your grandmother needs, please," she said to Sabine. "I'll get the door."

As Sabine balanced on one crutch and offered her ailing grandmother a glass of water, she could hear everything in the front room—from her mother's polite *"Guten abend"* to the visitor's *"Wie geht es ihnen?"* But as soon as the pleasantries of "Good evening" and "How are you?" were out of the way, the visitor got down to business.

"I understand about her weakness." The woman's voice sounded as if she did not—or maybe that she did understand, but didn't care. "However, your daughter still needs to attend classes *every* day. And I don't know why she refuses to join the *Junge Pioniere.* Perhaps you have not encouraged her?"

Obviously one of the *rektors* from her polytechnical *schule* had come. And she wanted Sabine to join the Young Pioneers? Perfect, if you liked Communist pep talks (like Comrade

Ulbricht's) or enjoyed shouting Communist slogans and parading the streets with flags and banners. No, thanks.

"It's just that—" Sabine's mother sounded far away. "Well, since the school year is over in just a few days, and she is so weak sometimes.... It's very hard for her, with her legs—"

Sabine didn't make a sound. But that's what it always came down to—her gimpy legs that refused to work the way they should. However, just this once, she didn't mind—as long as it kept her out of the Junge Pioniere.

Sabine noticed Oma Poldi had closed her eyes again. By the peaceful look on her impossibly wrinkled face, she hadn't heard a word.

"Beginning of year, end of year, there is no excuse. Weak or not, she *will* attend her classes more regularly, or else—"

The threat from the *rektor* hung in the air like thick smoke.

Or else what?

"She reads good books," Frau Becker put in. "Many good books. I believe she has learned as much from reading as... well, she is quite a bright girl."

"If she is as bright as you say, she will be wise to join in the Pioniere. And when she turns fourteen, she will go through the *Jugendweihe* dedication ceremony and graduate to the *Freie Deutsche Jugend.*"

Not the Free German Youth! Sabine wanted to yell. *I'm being confirmed in the church instead!*

"She'll receive very good training in the FDJ," added the *rektor.*

Brainwashing, you mean. Sabine bit her tongue to keep from yelling it.

"I will discuss it with her," Sabine's mother whispered.

"Discuss?" The visitor sounded like a lawyer in a courtroom. "You simply tell her what is expected, Comrade, and that will be the end of it. Most young people eagerly anticipate going through the *Jugendweihe.* They dedicate themselves to socialist ideals. Far superior to the old religious ceremonies, don't you agree?"

Frau Becker said nothing, but Sabine could almost hear her mother's teeth grinding.

"And what's this?" the woman went on. "You allow her to read *this* kind of book?"

Oh, no. Sabine winced, remembering that she had left *Black Beauty* on the table.

"Why, yes, I mean, no, I—," Sabine's mother stammered.

"You must know this is not an approved book."

Sabine could hear the poison dripping from the woman's words. "You don't want your child learning the wrong ideas, do you? Western propaganda?"

The wrong ideas? Sabine felt her ears starting to burn. The only wrong ideas she'd heard lately had come from her Communist teacher.

"I'll do you a favor, then." Suddenly the woman's voice sounded lighter. "I'll dispose of this book for you, and we'll just consider it a small mistake. But then I'll need your guarantee as a parent that Sabine will attend classes again tomorrow, without fail. Do we have an understanding?"

Sabine dared to peek around the door, just enough to see her mother standing with her back to the wall, biting her lip. Aunt Gertrud sat across the room, silent, knitting, a smile curling her lips. Her team was winning.

"Was I not clear, Frau Becker?" the teacher demanded.

"Ja, perfectly clear." Sabine's mother turned away, her shoulders slumped with defeat.

But that's my book! Sabine's mind screamed. Before she could change her mind, she swung herself into the room.

"Well!" The *rektor*'s eyes widened as she watched Sabine wobble-march straight toward her. "I thought perhaps you were resting. I hadn't expected to see you."

No, and the woman could not have expected the thirteen-year-old to rescue *Black Beauty.* Of course, Sabine had also surprised herself.

"Please pardon me for being rude." Sabine's heart beat wildly as she snatched her book and swallowed hard before backing up. "But I'd be happy to let you, um, *borrow* my book when I've finished reading it. The horse has just been sold to a new owner, you see, and I'd really like to know what happens next. Please excuse me."

She turned back toward the safety of Oma's room. She imagined the *rektor* gasping, or maybe that was Aunt Gertrud.

She stopped in the hallway but didn't dare turn around. "You don't have to worry. I'll be at school tomorrow."

There. She hid in Oma's room, barely daring to listen until their visitor had left. The front door slammed with a satisfying *thump*. Good.

"Sabine—" The girl jumped when her mother quietly rested a hand on her shoulder.

"I'm so sorry, Mama." The words tumbled out before she could stop them, but didn't they always? "I didn't mean to get you in trouble, but I just couldn't let her come in here and talk to you like that. When she said she was going to take my book, I—"

"Shh." Her mother gently turned Sabine around and touched a finger to her lips. "You don't want to wake Oma."

Oh. Right. Sabine whispered another apology. How many times could she say "I'm sorry"?

"Child, you don't need to apologize." Her mother leaned closer. "I'm the one who should apologize to you."

"For what? I know you do what you think is best. You work every day. You take good care of Oma. You let me stay home from school sometimes. You—"

"That's right, I do. But only because I feel guilty that you have to go to that horrible state school. All they want to do is train you to be a good Communist." But then she smiled, and for a second, her eyes sparkled. "But did you hear that poor woman? '*Black Beauty* is not on the approved list of books.' It's a horse story!"

Sabine proudly held up the treasure she'd rescued—for now. And they giggled together like sisters, two rebels with a cause. As long as they could keep their Bible and their books—

They sobered up quickly, though, when Oma Poldi groaned softly and stretched her chin and shoulders, as if waking up.

"I knew God had a reason for bringing us to the eastern side of the city." Sabine's mother looked down at her mother-in-law. She'd taken care of the woman every day for as long as Sabine could remember. They'd moved to Oma's apartment in the Russian-controlled sector of Berlin so long ago that Sabine couldn't remember living in the American sector. "And I still believe he does. Oma needs us. And her ties here are so strong. She raised her family in this apartment. You know her son, Erich's father, was a pastor here, and Oma still feels called to stay here. But Sabine, I often wonder if I did the right thing for *you* by bringing you here. Can you forgive me?"

Sabine squeezed her mother's hand.

"You don't have to worry about me, Mama. Sometimes I hate this place and the Vopos with their guns, keeping us here. But I don't believe a word of what they tell me in school."

Still the question nagged her: Why, exactly, had God brought *her* here? How could he use someone like her in a place like this?

As she shuffled out of the room, she promised herself that, no matter what, she would find the answer.

5

KAPITEL FÜNF

BARBED-WIRE SUNDAY

THREE MONTHS LATER...

At first, August 13, 1961, felt just like any other summer Sunday morning. The sun peeked through Sabine's window, waking her. She sat up on her cot and stretched. Soon she would have to be up and dressed, ready to walk with her mother to the church in the American sector. She shivered to think that Wolfgang the Watcher would surely notice and report them to the authorities again. Or worse. How long before they'd be arrested, the way so many others had been?

She hoped Erich would join them after his shift at the hospital. Puzzled, Sabine realized she didn't hear any movement from her mother's side of the room. No breathing or rustling. Nothing. She stared at the sheet that formed a curtain between their beds.

"Mama?" Sabine checked the mantel clock. *Seven-thirty, already!* "Are you awake?"

Still Sabine heard only steady snoring from the den, but that would be Uncle Heinz. More than once Sabine had thanked God that Oma Poldi's flat had a bedroom (for Oma), a sitting room (for her and Mama), and a den (for Aunt Gertrud and Uncle Heinz). Erich kept a bedroll in the corner, but half the time he slept at the hospital. So it wasn't unusual to see his roll folded and stowed in its place under the chair.

She reached for the curtain, not expecting to see her mother's sheets and blankets folded and stowed.

"Mama?" she whispered again, wondering where she'd gone. Feet pounded up the hall stairs, then to their front door. *The Vopo!* But Erich burst in, huffing and puffing.

"Get dressed, Sabine!" he ordered. "You're not going to believe what's going on out there!"

"What are you talking about?" Still shaken by her vision of being hauled away by the police, Sabine didn't move.

It took several tries for her breathless brother to explain in a way that made sense.

"Concrete posts. Barbed wire." His cheeks still flamed bright red. "Vopos all over with machine guns. They're running a fence right down the middle of Bernauerstrasse. They're really doing it! Right down the middle of Berlin!

"The *Volkspolizei* have even set up water cannons and machine guns on rooftops to keep the crowds away. Some folks are just curious, but lots are angry."

Sabine came to life and threw on some clothes, curious and a bit afraid to see the "People's Police" in action. Outside, Erich led the way through a cluster of quiet neighbors. They joined their mother, who looked stunned.

"Oh, Sabine." Frau Becker wrapped a protective arm around her daughter. "Sorry to leave you sleeping. Erich brought me down here about a half hour ago. I didn't want to wake you up if it turned out to be nothing."

But this was *something*. And Sabine could only stare in shock as the workers and Vopos and East German soldiers worked to put up an iron curtain between her world and the world outside.

"They cut off the U-Bahn at midnight," Erich told her quietly, turning away from the glare of a Vopo nearby. "Shut it down. Plus all the telephones, and streetcars, even pipelines. Nothing passes from East to West anymore. Or from West to East, either."

No more trips across the line to shop, to attend church, to visit friends, or even to hang out in the Tiergarten, a park Sabine loved.

"Too many people have managed to escape," whispered an older man standing next to them. Sabine could see his pajamas peeking out from underneath his clothes, and his gray hair stood straight up. "That's why they're caging us in. Like some kind of zoo animals, we are."

They all fell silent as a tractor lowered another concrete post into a hole in the middle of the street. Grim workers followed like spiders with their barbed-wire web, stringing it between posts set too close together for a person to squeeze through.

Sabine gasped as a half dozen West Berliners suddenly charged from the other side. The lead man held a shovel, as if to attack the new wall. Sabine gripped her crutch handles even more tightly.

"They're going to get killed!" she whispered. But the charge didn't even make it to the fence. Three Vopos with wickedly sharp bayonets on the ends of their Russian-made rifles blocked the advance. One of the soldiers shouted a warning before he fired into the air. And every eye on both sides of the new fence stared at the face-off. The six men skidded to a stop just inches from the tips of the bayonets.

The crowd gasped. Sabine's mother covered her daughter's hand with her own so tightly that Sabine could barely feel her fingers. Who would move first? A long moment later, the protesters raised their hands in surrender and backed away from the soldiers' threats. Most of the crowd gathered on their side of the new wall backed away too.

"You're not to go near those Vopos or that fence," Frau Becker warned her children. "Do you understand?"

Sabine nodded silently and tried to hide her angry tears. Yes, she understood. All too well. But how could they just stand back and let this happen?

"Why are they doing this to us?" Her voice rose a notch. Her mother tried to comfort her and lead her back home. Sabine stiffened and planted her crutches on the sidewalk. "And why didn't we leave before this thing went up?"

"Shh, Sabine. Now is not the time."

"No, now it's too late. We waited, and we waited. And now we'll never get out of here."

Erich joined their mother in steering Sabine back to the safety of home. But Sabine had to know.

"Why didn't we just take Oma with us? Why did we stay here with her? Look!"

"Sabine, shush."

"But, Mama! We should have—"

"You're getting worked up over something you can't change. I thought you understood. Your brother can't abandon his patients at the hospital. And Oma is very...determined to stay."

Determined? More like stubborn.

"Because?" But Sabine knew the answer.

"Because God placed her in this neighborhood. Maybe us, as well. You know she never asked us to stay. But we agreed that we would never abandon Oma."

Sabine knew Oma's faith led her to do what she believed, and her mother did the same. She wondered if she could be as trusting. But still she could not help staring over her shoulder at the ugly, frightening fence going up in the middle of their neighborhood. She could not help staring at the soldiers who defiantly pointed their guns and bayonets at them—as if she and her neighbors had done something wrong!

She wanted to curl up and cry, to run at the fence—screaming—as the brave but foolish men had, to throw a brick at the wall. Something! Anything! Instead, she let her mother and brother lead her home like a lamb, back to the apartment where Oma Poldi probably still slept.

When they checked on Oma, she hadn't even moved. A half hour later, Sabine left her mother and brother at the table to see if Oma wanted to eat yet.

"Oma?" she whispered, drawing a little closer. "Are you ready for a little breakfast?"

But Oma couldn't answer, and one side of her face looked funny. As she tried to sit up and speak, she slid off her pillow and nearly tumbled over the side of her bed.

"Oma!" Sabine nearly screamed as she grabbed Oma's sleeve to keep her from falling. "Erich! Come quick. There's something wrong with Oma!"

Later that night, Sabine paced outside the doors of St. Ludwig's Hospital, where Erich worked and Oma now rested. Not dead, *Gott sei Dank*. Thank God her mother had sent her in to see if Oma wanted breakfast.

"Are you sure you don't want to come inside and wait?" Erich called through the entrance. She could see his face in the little pool of light from the entry lamps. When she shook her head and kept walking, he jogged out to join her.

"Look, I know how you feel about this place. The bad memories and everything. That's why you won't come in, right?"

Oh, and she hadn't even told him the worst of it. She'd never told *anyone* about the worst days of her stay there. About the dark side of Nurse Ilse. About the beyond-painful therapy that the nurse seemed to enjoy. About the shouting and Nurse Ilse's threats. About the closet. Especially not about the closet. Even now she couldn't answer Erich.

"I'd probably feel the same way, if I were you."

But Nurse Ilse was long gone. Why did Sabine still feel so afraid? Finally she stopped, leaning on her crutches. Her big brother was only trying to help. And she had to know.

"Is Oma going to die?"

"Come on inside. The doctor explained everything to Mutti."

"I don't want to go inside to talk to Mama. Is she going to die? Just tell me!"

Erich raked his light hair off his forehead and leaned against the brick building. Yes, the air felt warm, but not warm enough for him to sweat like this.

"All right, listen. She had a stroke, and she's probably paralyzed. We don't know if she's going to live through the night. *That's* why you need to come inside."

"A *stroke*." Sabine repeated the word, wishing this day had never happened. First the horrible fence, then Oma. And now she couldn't stop shivering.

"So are you coming?" her brother asked.

Sabine crossed her arms and looked up at the hospital. A boy flattened his nose against a second-floor window, watching her through enormous black glasses. But a moment later, he'd disappeared. Erich looked up to see what had caused her questioning expression.

"Sabine?"

He hadn't seen the boy, maybe about her age, but downright skinny. His haunted look made Sabine shiver even more.

"Yes, I mean—" She stumbled over her words.

"So are you coming, or are you going to stand out here all night?"

When she studied the pain in her brother's face, she knew what she had to do—never mind the ghost of Nurse Ilse. She took a deep breath, nodded slowly, and started for the door.

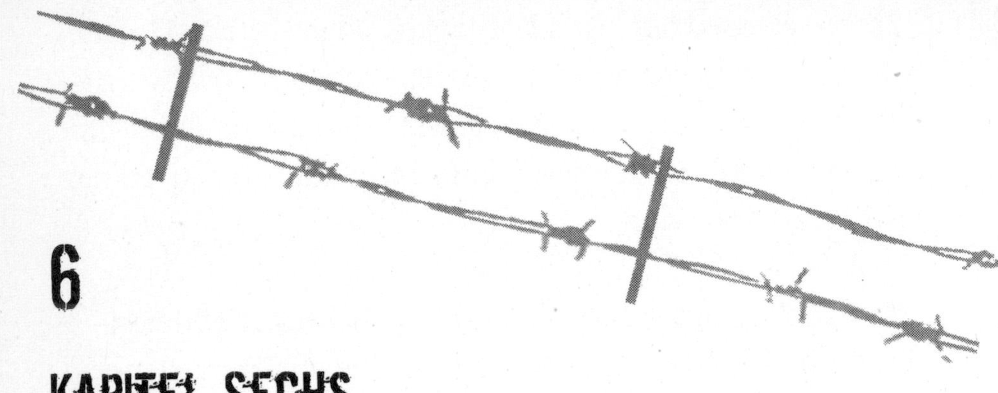

6

KAPITEL SECHS

OMA POLDI BECKER

Sabine's grandmother looked nearly the same as she always had, resting in bed, breathing quietly. She lay in the last bed in a row of ten, so when they came to visit they could see out the window to the street below. But after a day and a half, Oma had hardly opened an eye.

"Oma—" Sabine willed her grandmother to be well, to get out of the hospital bed. She wondered if Oma would ever speak to her again. She already felt a hole, once filled with Oma's warmth. They had smiled together, had shared secrets, and had prayed together.

And that was hard enough, but the hardest part—though Sabine would never admit it aloud—was seeing everyone in the hospital, and remembering. It seemed as if she had never left. When she closed her eyes, she felt the fear of Nurse Ilse's threats, of being imprisoned in the bed or the closet. She smelled the peculiar antiseptic the janitors used to mop the floor. She heard the squeaking of rubber-soled nurses' shoes in the hallways as they made their rounds, the muffled voices, and the clack of a typewriter down the hall. And she gripped Oma's iron bed railing to keep from fleeing.

Get out of here! Run. Walk. Crawl if you have to. Her head spun, and for a moment, she felt like she might pass out as she gasped for breath.

Footsteps approaching brought her back to the present, and she turned to see Erich, his white intern's smock flowing behind him. Pushing away her fear, she looked him in the eye and held her finger up to her mouth.

"Shh. Don't wake her up," Sabine whispered as she pointed to their mother, slumped on a waiting-room chair in the corner. Erich nodded and silently joined Sabine next to the bed.

If he saw it, he's not going to comment on my panic attack, she thought with relief.

"Onkel Heinz stopped by," he whispered. He bent a little closer to listen to Oma's breathing and checked his wristwatch. He wasn't a doctor, yet, but Sabine could tell he'd be a great one. "Mutti talked to him for a minute, but he left before you got here."

"Oh." Sabine didn't mind that she'd missed him. *Good.*

"He's still *celebrating* the new fence, that wall... if you can believe that." Erich shook his head in disgust. "As if it's something to get excited about."

"People are still escaping, though, aren't they?"

"Most people believe it's too dangerous, now." He lowered his voice further, as if someone might hear them. "The guards, the Vopos, they're crazy. Give them guns and they turn into monsters."

Sabine thought about what Erich said, then decided it wouldn't hurt—

"Erich, can I ask you something?"

He lifted an eyebrow. "If it's quick. I have to get back to Dr. Woermann's rounds. We're doing surgery this afternoon."

"Have you ever thought of trying to escape to the West?"

He brought a hand to his forehead, as if he'd been hit by a sudden headache.

"You're not serious, little sister."

"Yes, I am. The wall's made me really think about it, and what it means to be free, and I was just wondering if—"

"Hold on." He held up his hand for her to stop. "I don't think we should be talking about this right now."

Sabine had to lean toward him to hear.

"Why not?"

"Why not? Because you can get hurt. Just forget it. Don't even talk about it. There are too many—" He sighed. "There are too many ways to get in trouble asking those kinds of questions. But listen, when Mutti wakes up, tell her I'll be home late tonight."

"Aren't you always?"

He winked at her and hurried off, the big brother, the doctor-to-be, leaving her once again with her fears. She suddenly realized he hadn't answered her question.

"Our apartment building is right next to the new wall," said a voice in the shadows, which made her jump. "You should see it. They woke us up Saturday night, when they started pounding in the street and putting up the posts."

"Oh! You nearly gave me a heart attack."

"Sorry. But we're in the right place for that, aren't we?"

Is that supposed to be funny? Sabine couldn't see who belonged to the voice, then a boy about her age stepped out of the shadows. He squinted at her from behind an enormous pair of black-rimmed glasses. And then she knew.

"You're the kid in the window," she told him. "I saw you staring at me and my brother the other night."

"Me?" He wrinkled his forehead as if trying to remember. "I wasn't staring."

"You were too staring."

"Well, then not on purpose."

"You were staring accidentally?"

"My mother's here, and I visit her a lot," he told Sabine. "I just look outside sometimes to pass the time."

"Oh. And you make big spots on the window with your nose too."

"Well, I didn't see anybody," he said defensively.

Sabine hadn't noticed how thick the boy's glasses were until he turned away.

"Wait a minute." She held up her hand. "Are those glasses . . . I mean, can you—"

"See? Hardly. If I take them off, I'm practically blind."

"What about with them on?"

"With them on, I'm practically blind."

He chuckled and pointed at her crutches.

"What about those things? Are you—"

"Disabled? You should see me try to walk without them."

"Can you?"

"Not really," Sabine admitted.

"Are you a patient here?"

"Used to be. But I haven't been back here since I was a little girl. I'm here visiting my grandmother. My name's Sabine, by the way. Sabine Becker."

"And I'm Willi Stumpff. Nice to meet you."

"Did you say your mother's here?"

"Yep. She had a baby, but it came too early. Mom had a hard time with the baby, and the doctors want to keep an eye on her while she heals. They're not sure about my little sister, either."

"Wow. I'm sorry." She looked over at Oma again.

"Ja. Everybody in my family is praying for her, but—" He chuckled again and looked around, as if somebody might be spying on them.

"But what?"

"But you'd better not tell my Junge Pioniere leader. I think he believes Christians are dumb or something."

"You're in the Pioniere, and you're a Christian? What about all that hip-hooray they do at their meetings, listening to all that Communist 'for peace and socialism' stuff?"

He chuckled again, and the big glasses slid down his nose. "It's just easier that way. If you knew my parents, you'd know what I mean. I'm not a Communist, though. Just don't tell anybody, or I might get into trouble."

So why is he telling me, a stranger?

As they talked some more, Sabine decided she liked Willi Stumpff's openness. She learned that he and his family attended the Lutheran church, which helped explain about the people praying for his mother. And it didn't take long to figure out that he really couldn't see much farther than ten feet. That explained why he'd seemed to stare right at her the other night but hadn't recognized her close up.

"So you can't really see what's going on outside your window?"

"I can hear things really good. Like—"

He paused and pulled her to the side.

"Like the nurse coming up behind us," he whispered. "She's a Communist, and you should stay out of her way."

Oh. Sabine didn't look as the woman in uniform hurried past.

"I can see shapes okay," he went on. "My mama sometimes tells me what she sees. Or she did, before the baby came and she had to stay here. She describes things so well, it seems like I can see them too."

"So what do you ... I mean, what does your mother see out your window at home?"

"Oh, we have a great view of the Spree River, and the new fence runs right below us. You know, the wall they're starting to build. You can practically touch it."

"Wow. I can't imagine what it would be like to need someone to tell you what's right outside your own window."

"Guess I can't imagine needing crutches to get around," Willi responded. So there. Maybe they had a lot more in common than either realized at first.

"Yeah." Sabine smiled. "I guess having crutches makes it a little harder to drive."

"You mean like a car?" Willi's eyes widened in surprise. He didn't know her well enough to know she was joking. But come on, they were only thirteen, right?

"Army staff car." She folded her arms and nodded. "Volkswagen. It's mine."

Well, technically, maybe ... not. Unless you lived by the law of finders-keepers. But she didn't tell him that part. And his eyes started to look like magnified saucers as she described the underground bunker and "her" car. She neglected to mention some of the minor details, like the missing wheels and the engine that sort of lay in pieces on the ground. Other than that, she could probably drive it right out of there, if she wanted to.

"Really?" Willi still couldn't believe it. "This I have to see."

She thought for a moment. Could she really trust this boy? Then again, he'd trusted her from the start.

"Maybe—" She hesitated. "But on one condition."

"Name it."

"That you don't tell anybody."

He nodded. "No problem."

"And then," she added, "you have to let me see what the city looks like from your window."

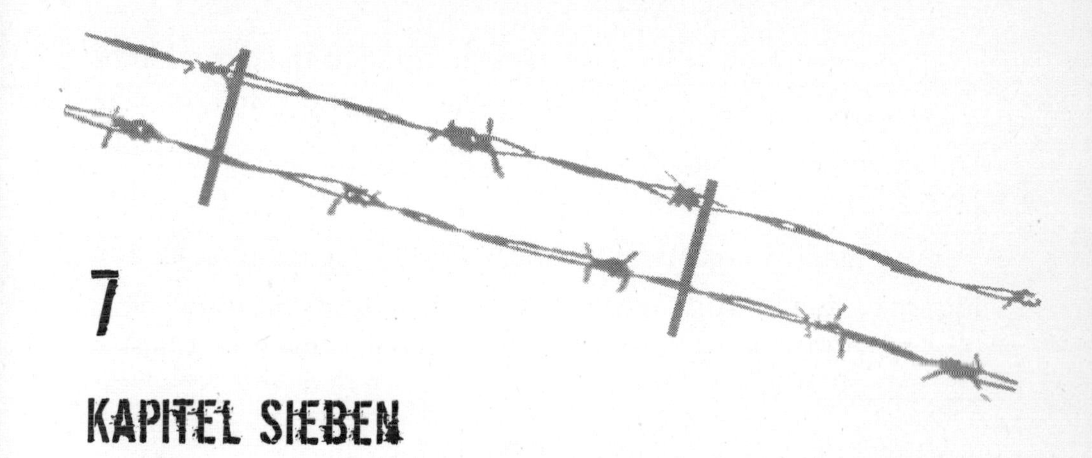

7

KAPITEL SIEBEN

THE VIEW FROM WILLI'S PLACE

The following afternoon, Sabine stood in Willi Stumpff's fifth-floor apartment, staring out the window at the divided city and the Spree River.

"What a great view. I've never seen a better one. And it looks totally different up here," she told him, "compared to down on the street. The East and West sides of Berlin look like different worlds from up here!"

Willi nodded as if he agreed, though she wasn't sure. He couldn't see the new buildings and shops on the other side of the fence and the bombed-out buildings on their side. Could he? The bright signs and lights on the other side, the gray on their side. It was almost as if the war had never ended in half of the city.

And they were in the wrong half.

"I used to play in that park." She pointed at the green acres of Tiergarten, now forbidden territory, just across the river. And again she almost forgot that Willi couldn't see what she did.

"You mean Tiergarten? Me too." He nodded, running a finger across the worn velvet of a rich red drape. She'd never seen him at the park. Maybe rich kids like him went to different schools.

"What does your father do?" she asked Willi. "I didn't see him at the hospital."

"Oh." His face fell. "Well, yeah, I don't see him much, either. He used to work for the government. Now he works on cars."

Nothing wrong with that. But the way Willi said it made her feel as if it were, well, embarrassing. Willi's father paced in the next room, talking on the telephone in hushed tones. Sabine wished she hadn't asked.

But Willi seemed to shrug it off. He pressed his nose to the window as he had at the hospital. Without taking his eyes from the view, he asked her to describe everything she could see.

"Everything?" She wondered whether she'd get home for dinner in time. When he nodded, she started by telling him about the people walking through the park and the people riding bicycles along their side of the border. She told him about the little shops on both sides of the fence, about the church and the graveyard. She described the soldiers patrolling with guns and the men laying a brick wall next to the barbed-wire fence.

"And look there!" She waved one arm wildly while balancing her crutches with the other.

"What are you doing?" Willi grabbed her wrist and tried to pull her away from the window. "Someone's going to see you!"

"That's the point!" She wrestled her arm free. "I see a couple of American soldiers, over on the other side of the fence... Yoo-hoo! Over here!"

Willi held his head in his hands and looked alarmed. But never mind him. And never mind that his father would probably hear her. She continued to wave as wildly as she could, hoping to catch the Americans' attention.

"There, see? They're stopping!" She waved again, just in case one of the soldiers happened to look up. She prayed the American soldiers could do something about their prison city. Her brother had told her stories about when he was her age, when the American planes flew into the city, bringing food and coal, even candy for the kids.

But that was a long time ago, and these were not the same soldiers. They wore the same uniforms, though, with the same pretty red, white, and blue flag on their jeep. *Come on, look up!*

But a moment later, she let her hand fall.

"What happened? Did they see you?" Willi still hid behind his hands. "Do they have guns? Are they looking up here?"

"Willi, they're Americans, not the Stasi." Not the feared secret state police. She watched, disappointed, as they started their jeep. "Aww. There they go. They just stopped to talk to somebody down there."

She watched the Americans until they had driven out of sight, up their side of Bernauerstrasse.

"See anything else?" Willi finally asked after she'd stayed quiet for a few minutes.

Ja, she did. She continued telling him about the people outside the window: A couple trying to maneuver a baby carriage over a curb. A serious-looking man in a dark gray coat (even in the summer heat!)...probably a secret agent. That's what secret agents wore. She even told Willi about the couple strolling close to the fence, and—

"Wait a minute. He's walking right toward the fence." *What was he doing?*

"What? Do you mean he's trying to—"

"I think so." She nodded. She didn't even need to say the word *escape.* They both knew.

"What about the woman? You said they were a couple."

"She's grabbing his arm, like she doesn't want him to go."

"But he's going anyway?"

Sabine lowered her voice, hoping Willi might do the same. She didn't want Herr Stumpff to come investigate.

"He just shook her off. Now he's trying to climb over the barbed wire."

"What about the guards?"

"One of them is—" The words just wouldn't come. They'd all heard World War 2 stories about the Nazis, the Blackshirts, the Brownshirts, the villains, the men who blindly followed Hitler. Now here in the People's German Democratic Republic,

Soviet-controlled East Germany, they had Vopos. The men who knocked on doors in the middle of the night, who kept people from escaping to freedom in the West. The men now pointing their guns at the man trying to scale the fence.

"Are you sure he's trying to escape?" Willi leaned against the window as if he could see for himself. "It's not even night yet. He must be crazy."

Sabine nodded but could not take her eyes off the scene below.

"Come on, Sabine. You have to tell me."

But Sabine's throat had gone dry, and she could barely speak. "He, he's...climbing, now. The woman is on her knees on the sidewalk. I think she's crying. Motioning to him. Telling him to stop, probably."

"And?"

"Another guard just ran over."

"He's got a gun?"

Sabine nodded.

"Sabine?"

"Yeah. He's...pointing his gun. He's—"

She winced. A muffled *pop-pop,* like fireworks from a distance, reached them. Seconds, maybe a minute ticked by before Willi spoke again.

"Do you think he's alive?" he wondered quietly.

"There's an ambulance down there. They're carrying him off." *Did he move? Maybe.* "I think maybe he is. It looked like he moved his arm. I think."

Or she prayed that he did. Suddenly she hated the wall that now divided their city: allowing free people on one side, trapping people on the other. The free could travel and laugh and buy things in the West; the trapped faced dreary gray cement apartment buildings and limited supplies in the East. No wonder the man had risked his life.

Sabine's shocked tears had begun to dry, and she gripped her crutches until her hands turned white. Wasn't this the kind of thing Corrie ten Boom and Anne Frank had lived through? She'd read books about both of them—books that weren't likely on the "approved" list. Maybe World War 2 hadn't really ended sixteen years earlier, in 1945. Maybe she had just seen it begin again, right outside Willi Stumpff's fifth-floor window.

Sabine couldn't watch anymore. She wanted to throw up. And she hadn't realized it before, but she'd bitten her lip so hard that now she could taste the blood.

"I have to go," she finally told Willi. He didn't ask about seeing her car. Good. Some other time, maybe.

"See you at St. Ludwig's tomorrow?" he asked. He looked as shaken as she felt.

She nodded.

Maybe tomorrow.

8

KAPITEL ACHT

THE IDEA

"I've been thinking, Willi." Sabine leaned against the wall, near the empty nurses' station.

"That's scary."

"No, really. I think I know how the last war happened."

"Let's hear it for the world-famous Sabine." He raised his voice like a circus announcer. "The girl who's unlocked the key to world peace."

"You're making jokes. I'm serious." She checked to make sure no one was listening.

"Oh, you want a good joke? How about this one: When does a Trabi reach top speed?"

"Willi, I don't think—"

"Come on; it's just a car joke. When does it go the fastest?"

She sighed. "I give up."

"When it's being towed away."

He cackled as if his joke about the clunky East German car were the funniest thing he'd ever heard, but he stopped when he saw Sabine's halfhearted grin.

"Sorry. You were telling me about world peace. Go ahead."

"Listen—" Sabine held up her finger like an Einstein who had just come up with the Big Answer, maybe a cure for cancer. "It wasn't that there weren't enough good people. The problem was that they were all too afraid to speak up."

"That's it?" Willi raised his eyebrows at her.

"Right." She nodded. "And the same thing's happening today. Everybody's too scared to say anything about the wall. But if we all worked together, we could stop it."

"We could, huh? How?"

She scratched her head.

"I haven't figured that part out yet. But I do know how we can bring people together. Right now they're just standing around watching the wall go up, acting like a bunch of sheep."

"Baa."

"Would you quit it?" She punched him on the shoulder. "Do you want to stop the wall, or don't you?"

"You know I don't like it any more than you do." He sighed. "We used to visit my cousins in the American sector and my grandparents. Everybody's over there, and we're stuck over here for the rest of our lives."

Sabine told him her plan, but he didn't seem convinced.

"What if somebody finds out?" he asked. "Do you know how much trouble we'd be in?"

"First of all, nobody's ever going to find it down in the bunker. And second of all, if Anne Frank could do it, so can we!"

"Who's Anne Frank? Somebody you know?"

"You're kidding me. You didn't read that book?"

He shrugged. And for a moment, she wondered if boys had half a brain.

"It's this diary, see, and—"

"I'm not into girls' diaries. Boys write journals."

"Would you stop? I'm trying to explain. Anne Frank was Jewish, and she had to hide in someone's attic the whole war, and she was really brave, and she wrote a diary, which they turned into a book. Got it now?"

"Got it. So we write a journal."

"No. I'm just saying she was brave, even when people were out to get her."

"Oh." Willi scratched his head. "Okay."

"So tomorrow night we meet in the bunker, and we don't tell anybody else."

He raised his right hand. "On my honor as a Junge Pioniere."

"Ohhh." She rolled her eyes. "Anything but that."

"Scout's honor, then."

"You're not a Scout. How do you know what they do?"

"They have them in England. And America. They go camping. I read it somewhere."

"I thought you didn't read."

"I do too. Just not girls' diaries."

"All right. But forget the Pioneer honor." She held out her hand for him to shake. "We have to make a pact."

"Sounds serious." He wasn't smiling anymore. "What kind of pact?"

"To do whatever we can, for as long as we can. For freedom."

Willi rubbed his chin and thought for a moment, then nodded and shook her hand. "For freedom," he said, echoing her words. Time to get down to business.

"So how much money do you have?" she asked him. "We're going to need it to make this plan work."

And the plan would work just fine, as long as Uncle Heinz didn't hear her leave the apartment.

"Who's that?" he mumbled from his dark corner.

Sabine quietly pulled her little backpack on, glad no one had turned on the light.

"Just Sabine," she whispered. "I'm going down the hall."

Which was true, and nighttime visits to the washroom at the end of the hall weren't unusual. She waited a moment at the door, wondering if her uncle would respond. He just grunted and launched back into his snoring. Good. Now she just had to get out of the building and down the street without anybody else stopping her.

"You'd better be there, Willi Stumpff," she whispered as she slipped onto the dark street. The stairs didn't stop her, though she had to admit it took her a little longer to take them one at a time. But now she didn't stop long enough to let goose bumps climb the back of her neck. She just might turn around and scurry back to bed rather than make her way to the bombed-out apartment building on Bergstrasse.

What was that? Someone coming down the street? Sabine dived into the shadows, crutches and all. A dog barked, and a door slammed.

But no one came toward her.

After a minute, she breathed again and picked up her back-pack. *Keep going. There it is.* She slipped through the crumbled entry and felt her way into the maze of rooms.

"Willi?" she whispered. Losing her concentration for a moment, she tripped over a loose brick but caught herself before falling on her face. When she looked up, she could make out a flickering light up ahead.

"So I finally get to see this car of yours," Willi announced from the shadows. Light from his candle glittered and reflected off his glasses, casting weird shapes on the broken walls around them.

"There you are," she greeted him. "I was afraid you weren't going to show."

"Didn't I say I would be here?"

"Yeah, but—"

"Or did you think I was too blind to find my way around the neighborhood?"

"You said it, not me."

He just smiled and pulled a little round compass out of his pocket, holding it up to the light.

"I don't get too lost. But where's your car?"

"All right, Mr. Boy Scout." She led the way to the trapdoor. Five minutes later, Willi walked all around the Volkswagen, leaning closer with the candle for a better look.

"Whoa." He whistled. "Too bad it doesn't have an engine, or wheels, or a windshield, or... let's see. What *does* it have?"

"It has seats. But now you've seen it. Did you bring the stuff?"

"Patience. I brought it." He unloaded his own small backpack. "One hundred eighty-seven sheets of paper. That's all I could find in my father's office. And the ink. What about you?"

Sabine pulled out her box.

"It has three different sizes of letters, and they snap together like this, see?" She showed him how the printing kit worked, the one she'd bought with Willi's money at the *Schreibwarenhandlung.* The stationery store owner had even shown her how to work it. "First, you arrange all the little rubber letters into words. Next, you ink the letters up with the roller, then you press it against the paper like so."

"An underground printing press."

"Just like in this book I read about the Danish underground movement," she told him as she started sorting letters. "They did this kind of thing during World War Two."

"Another book, huh?" He picked up one of the novels she'd left in the car before tossing it back. "Let's just figure out what we're going to say and get out of here."

"How about *Liebe Freiheit, Keine Mauer*?" Sabine asked.

" 'Up with Freedom, Down with the Wall!' Yeah, I like it."

Sabine set up the headline while Willi worked on the rest.

"Done yet?" she asked him five minutes later.

"Come on. You just have four words. I have forty."

"You can do it."

"Didn't say I couldn't. How about this: 'We must protest until the wall comes back down.' Does that sound—"

"Perfect." And for the next hour, they printed sheet after sheet of their protest papers.

"Hey, we're getting pretty good at this," Willi told her as they worked their way through the paper supply.

Well, sort of. Some looked smudged, others crooked, but they kept working. Roll ink on the letters, press against the paper, peel it off... paper after paper.

Willi brought his hand up to meet a yawn, and Sabine giggled. Even in the candlelight, she could see the inky fingerprints on his cheek.

"We're done," Sabine announced as she pulled the last paper off. "Do you know what time it is?"

"Don't know; don't want to know." Willi gathered a handful of papers. "Let's just get this over with. But—" He hesitated. "What about that guy, Wolfgang, who's always watching you from his apartment window?"

"What about him? Most of the time he's there; sometimes he's not."

"Have you actually ever met him?"

"You don't want to know, Willi." She pushed away the memory of Wolfgang waiting for her at the foot of the stairs.

"Well, maybe he's asleep."

And maybe not. Sabine just followed Willi up the stairway and back to her neighborhood. She held her breath, but Wolfgang's window looked dark; nothing moved.

"Up there?" Willi followed her gaze, and she nodded. If Wolfgang were watching, well... Sabine squared her shoulders and prayed he wasn't. They still had work to do.

Their first stop: the townhouse apartments down her street. Sabine felt a tingle as she slipped the first few leaflets under the doors. What would people think when they read them?

Willi had crossed to the other side of the street, working his way toward Sabine's apartment at twice her speed.

Willi! She wanted to scream but could only freeze in terror and melt into a dark doorway. A Vopo policeman had rounded a corner, and Willi had stumbled right into his path. Though the boy wiggled and protested, the Vopo held him tightly. Sabine's heart nearly beat out of her chest as she tried to think.

But Willi acted; he planted a good kick in one of the man's shins—just enough to loosen his grip. In a heartbeat, Willi whirled free and sprinted down the sidewalk, leaving the policeman in a cloud of flying protest papers.

"Halt!" The Vopo drew his gun, but he was still hopping in pain. Willi had already darted around a corner.

Sabine stared in amazement. That kid could get around! He couldn't see clearly ten feet in front of his own face, but he could run like the wind.

Sabine's grin melted, and she nearly choked when the Vopo seemed to look straight at her, as if he could hear her heart beating.

Could he? She stood lamppost-still in the dark, not breathing, not blinking. She still clutched the "Up with Freedom, Down with the Wall!" papers that would send her straight to jail. She could only watch as the man lit a match and held it to a stack of their papers. When he seemed satisfied that they would burn, he tossed the whole lot in the gutter.

Sabine buried her face in the brick wall as a flickering light groped the shadows. Surely he would discover her. She waited silently, the blood pounding in her ears, the sound of the Vopo's laugh echoing down the street. She could not fight and run, the way Willi had. But maybe if she screamed someone would help her. Maybe Mama would even hear her. Armed with a plan, she turned to face the Vopo—

Who had disappeared. She caught her breath and looked down the street.

No one. All he'd left behind were paper ashes and a few embers, flickering orange reminders of their protest. She walked over and poked the burned pile with her crutch. All that work—

Sadly, she straightened up and instinctively looked over her shoulder at Wolfgang's window. Did the curtain move? She didn't wait to check. She and Willi would just have to think of a better way to get people's attention.

She just had to slip back into her apartment without waking anyone up. She couldn't help yawning as she realized how long she'd been awake. This felt like the longest trip down the hall she'd ever made. As she quietly entered the apartment, she immediately knew something wasn't right.

Aunt Gertrud's voice hissed out of the darkness. "Where have you been all this time?"

Sabine squinted as the probing beam of a flashlight searched out her face. At least she'd slipped the leftover flyers into her backpack.

"Oh, it's you." Sabine yawned like Miss Innocent, ignoring her aunt's question. "I was just going back to bed."

"You most certainly were not down the hall all this—" began Aunt Gertrud. Another sleepy voice interrupted.

"Sabine?" her mother asked. "What's all the noise?"

"Sorry to wake you," Sabine whispered as she used the chance to get into her bed. She pulled the sheets to her chin and decided she could take off her shoes later. Hugging her backpack under the sheets, she closed her eyes.

With a disgusted sigh, Aunt Gertrud switched off the flashlight and shuffled back to bed.

And Sabine did her best to keep from shaking.

9

KAPITEL NEUN

VISIT FROM THE STASI

"What about all the printing stuff?" asked Willi, and Sabine shushed him. She waited a moment while a doctor hurried by, his white smock rustling.

"It's still safe down in the bunker, if we need it again."

"What?" Willi leaned closer to hear.

"I *said*—"

A hospital orderly gave them a curious look as he walked by pushing a laundry cart. Sabine recognized him, one of her brother Erich's friends. Dietrich, wasn't it? He smiled at them. But after a quick nod, she turned away so he wouldn't hear her response to Willi.

"Listen," she said as she pulled him back into a corner stacked high with white sheets and thin blue hospital blankets. "We have to come up with a better plan."

"Yeah," he agreed. "That was a little too close last—"

"Hey, there you are!" Erich walked up and ruffled Sabine's hair. She'd tried to duck but was too late.

"What do the doctors say about Oma?" she asked, not sure she wanted the real answer.

Erich's shoulders fell a bit.

"You see her, same as the doctors. She's getting a little worse each day. But she's hanging on—"

Sabine nodded. She kept hoping the news would change for the better.

"Can you do me a favor?" he asked. "I need you to carry a message home for me."

Sabine couldn't help yawning as she nodded.

"Late night, huh? Well, just tell Mutti that I have to work a bit late, but I should be home by seven. Can you remember that?"

"By seven," she repeated. *Late again?*

Dietrich came back down the hall, this time with his arms full of blankets.

"Hey, back to work!" he teased, a smile breaking through his long face. "Or have we gone on strike today?"

"That's it!" Sabine snapped her fingers and grabbed Willi's arm. "I don't know why I didn't think of it!"

"Did I say something?" Dietrich asked them.

"Gotta go," Sabine said. She tugged on Willi's sleeve and started toward the exit. She stopped only long enough to wave to Erich and the puzzled orderly.

"Already I don't like it," Willi protested, following her. He tried to put on the brakes when they got to the street, but

Sabine had set her course and had no intention of slowing down.

"You can't not like it. You haven't even heard my idea."

"I don't need to hear it. I just know that it's going to get us in trouble, like we were in last night."

"Oh, come on. Remember our pact? This is foolproof. Now, here's the plan—"

A half hour later, Sabine repeated the steps in her head as they neared their first target. They'd find plenty of people, probably cranky in the summer heat, standing in lines this time of day. For eggs, one line. For meat, another line. For carrots, yet another line. Working people, on their way home. Perfect. But could she convince Willi?

"You really think everybody's just going to agree? 'Yeah, that's a great idea, we hate the wall too.' Why would they go along with this—"

"This brilliant idea?" she finished. She stepped aside as an older woman hurried out a shop door, bells tinkling. "Of course they'll go along with it. Everyone hates the way we live in this half of Berlin. Everyone hates these lines. And everyone hates the wall. All they need is someone to tell them what to do."

"Baa." Willi did his sheep imitation just under his breath, and Sabine elbowed him as they entered the shop. But he knew what to do, and like a good soldier, he shuffled into one of the lines. Sabine took her place in the other.

At the front of Sabine's line, a squat, frowning man studied his tiny piece of sausage. The butcher hadn't given him enough meat to feed a toy poodle. And so Sabine made her first move, planting one of her crutches far enough into the aisle to trip the retreating customer.

"Entschuldige!" she whispered, afraid to look up. "Excuse me. But did you hear about the strike tomorrow? No one is going to work. To protest the... wall."

What else could she say? The man's worn leather shoes paused for a moment next to her crutch then stepped carefully around and continued out the door. When she finally looked up, Willi shrugged and gave her an "oh, well" look. His turn came as a middle-aged woman approached from the head of his line.

"We're having a strike," he blurted out, way too loudly. A couple of people turned, eyebrows raised, and his cheeks flamed red—as if he'd just belched, or worse. "That is, I mean—"

The woman breezed by him. But an older woman ahead of him crossed her arms and turned to face him. She seemed almost as wide as she was tall.

"What are you babbling about, boy?"

He glanced at Sabine before taking a deep breath to answer.

"A strike. You know. No working. To protest... lousy food. And the w-w-wall."

The woman just glared at him for a long moment, then she harrumphed and turned her back on him.

And so it went: at the *metzgerladen* that had little meat, at the *bäckerei* that offered little bread, at the *milchladen* that had almost no milk. When Sabine and Willi got kicked out of one shop, they tried another. And another. But in the end, it didn't seem to matter. Sabine grew more and more discouraged as everyone responded like sheep, sheep, sheep.

"What is wrong with these people?" she demanded. After an hour, even Sabine had to admit that her plan wouldn't work.

"I don't know." Willi shook his head and started counting on his fingers. "I had about a dozen people walk by like I didn't exist, even more who just growled or gave me what I can only guess were dirty looks, and at least eight who threatened to call the police."

"And you did better than I did." Sabine batted a chunk of concrete from the sidewalk with her crutch, sending it skittering into the *strasse* like a hockey puck. "But at least we didn't get thrown in jail."

"Well, I don't know about you, Sabine, but I'm done." He turned off at his corner. "Pact or no pact. Maybe I'll see you at the hospital tomorrow."

She nodded and let her shoes drag on the sidewalk, even though her mother always told her not to. It scuffed the sides and the toes. Maybe she would just end up like Anne Frank—captured by the soldiers in the end. As she rounded the corner of her floor's hallway, she froze at the sight of two men in dark leather coats leaving Frau Finkenkrug's apartment.

Stasi! One of them slammed the door shut.

"Republikflucht," muttered the other one, a tall man with a goatee just like Comrade Ulbricht's. They obviously hadn't noticed Sabine—yet. So she backed up as quickly as she dared. Before she backed around the corner, she silently watched the men apply an official-looking red seal to the wood just above the doorknob. It was obviously meant to keep anyone from opening the apartment again soon. As if Frau Finkenkrug had come down with some kind of terrible sickness, like smallpox or black death.

But Sabine knew better. She liked the sound of that word: *Republikflucht.* Flight from the Republic. The frau had escaped! And it would sound even better if people would say it of her and her mother.

"Come on," she heard one of the men say. "We're going to be here all night if we don't get these interviews done soon."

She heard the men rap sharply on Herr Gruhn's door, hardly waiting for the old man to answer before they pushed their way inside. Sabine knew the pattern: the Stasi would search each apartment, looking until they found something they could use as an excuse to arrest someone, to blame that person for helping the frau escape. A radio tuned to the wrong station? A piece of forbidden *Westliteratur,* like a magazine from the other side of the border? That would be enough. Sabine shivered. When she heard Herr Gruhn's door close, she hurried past it to her door.

"Mama!" she whispered as she pushed inside. "Your fashion magazines! They're coming!"

Frau Becker dropped her spoon in the soup kettle and ran to snatch up the forbidden literature. Sabine could think of nothing more silly than hiding magazines from the Stasi. She hardly had time to grab two magazines off the table and replace them with a couple of Communist brochures—the kind Uncle Heinz brought home from his tractor factory—before the familiar sharp knock on the door made her jump.

"*Um Himmels willen*!" Aunt Gertrud declared, stumbling out of the front room. She looked as if she'd just rolled out of bed. "Heavens! Who is making all that noise?"

She froze in horror when the two Stasi pushed the door open.

"Aack!" She grabbed at her hair and spun around to scurry through the doorway.

"Excuse me," Frau Becker said, "but that door was closed."

"We knocked," said the man with the goatee. He barged into the kitchen and inspected the Communist brochures. Hmm, that made a good first impression, but maybe not good enough. Sabine gripped her mother's magazines behind her back and leaned against the wall. Had one of these men stopped Willi last night?

Too bad Uncle Heinz was out with his friends at the pub.

"My husband and I are loyal party members," stated Aunt Gertrud as she returned to the room, her hair swept into a hasty bun. But they only waved her off as they yanked several books from the bookshelf and let them drop to the floor.

"If you're looking for something—" Sabine's mother didn't have any better luck talking to the men. Finally the taller man straightened up and stared straight at Sabine.

"You knew the woman down the hall, didn't you? Finkenkrug?"

Sabine felt her mouth go dry, but she managed to nod.

"Then you knew she was planning to defect." The statement sounded like an accusation.

"No, she didn't," her mother responded. "How would a child know such things?"

He dropped another pile of books to the floor, never taking his eyes off Sabine.

"Your older brother, the intern. Where is he? He's not at the hospital."

"What do you know about my son?" But the question only brought a frown from the Stasi interrogator.

"You tell him we will be back to speak with him. We have a few questions for him."

"My husband can help," offered Aunt Gertrud, but the men ignored her. They turned together to leave, as if pulled by the same leash. The tall one neatly stepped over a pile of books on his way to the door.

"You tell him," he repeated, pausing only long enough to see Frau Becker's white-faced nod.

And that's when Sabine knew—more than ever—that they could not stay in this place.

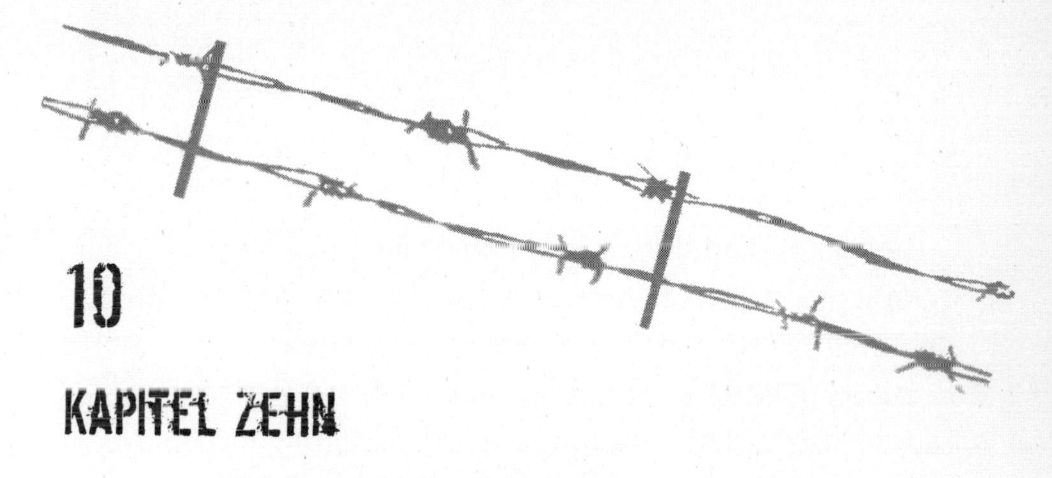

10

KAPITEL ZEHN

AN UNEXPECTED FRIEND

"Do you know that guy?" Willi whispered as they walked the hospital hall from his mother's room to Sabine's grandmother's. Sabine glanced to the side without moving her head.

"Oh." She returned the smile. "That's just Dietrich, Erich's friend."

"So what was the thumbs-up for?"

"I have no idea."

As they passed the nurses' station, a college-aged girl in a white trainee's uniform looked up from her clipboard and winked.

"Good work, you two," she whispered, just loud enough for them to hear as they walked by.

"Pardon me?" Sabine stopped short. The nurse's aide cautiously checked the hallway before she reached into her pocket and pulled out a folded piece of paper.

"This." She hardly had to show it to them; they'd spent enough hours printing their flyers to recognize it. "It was a good thought. But maybe you should be a little more careful next time."

Willi looked as stunned as Sabine felt.

"Another friend of your brother's?" he wondered, and the aide smiled at them as if expecting the question.

"Sorry to be so mysterious," she told them, her voice still low. "I'm Greta. There's a group of us here at the hospital. We get together for a Bible study every week. I guess you could say we stick together."

"So how do you know about us, and—" Sabine wasn't sure how to finish the question without admitting everything. But something about Greta's friendly expression made it easy to trust her.

"Well, for one thing, you and your friend talk a lot here in the hospital. I'd be a little more careful if I were you."

"Oh." Sabine felt her cheeks go red, and she glared at Willi with the big mouth. He looked as if he had no idea what Greta meant. As in, *Who, me?*

"Don't worry about it. Just find something else to talk about. Not everybody here at the hospital is on our side."

And what side is that? Sabine wanted to ask.

Greta went on in her low voice. "Besides that, your brother tries to keep track of you, you know. He thinks you might get into trouble."

"Who, me?"

Greta nodded. "*Ja*, and he wouldn't want me to say anything to you, but"—her smile had disappeared—"we need to ask you about something—"

A doctor approached them, obviously looking for something—or someone. When he motioned for the aide to follow him, Greta pinched her lips together and nodded. Right away, of course.

She pointed at them as she left. "Don't go anywhere." The young aide hurried after the doctor, leaving Sabine and Willi to wonder.

"What was *that* all about?" asked Willi. Sabine could only shrug her shoulders as they made their way to Oma's room.

"I have no idea," she finally said as they neared her door. "But maybe she was right. Maybe we do need to be more careful."

"I thought we already *were*. Didn't you?"

This time Sabine didn't answer. She paused to take a breath, praying that God would keep her, once again, from screaming and fleeing this place. It wouldn't take much to send her running.

She looked at the unscrubbed floor and the beds filled with sick and dying people. The limp sheet showed that man's missing left leg. She tried not to see the woman with the black, sunken eyes who, day after day, stared silently at the ceiling and waited to die. Sabine tried not to look at any of them. Finally they came to Oma's bed, last in line. But her heart sank when she looked at her grandmother. Sabine kept thinking that maybe, if she prayed a little harder, Oma would look better, not so frail.

Was this really the same Oma she had known all her life? This woman lay curled like a helpless baby, her cheeks hollow as if she hadn't eaten in weeks. The left side of her face sagged as if it had been painted on a wet canvas and the colors had all run.

The Oma she knew had fiery eyes that grabbed you and wouldn't let go. This woman looked from one face to the next, confused and frightened.

She didn't even sound like Oma. This woman moved her lips and groaned, forcing out jumbled bits of words.

"Hi, Oma. Sorry I couldn't come see you yesterday." Sabine tried not to let her emotions show. She reached out to take her grandmother's hand. Slowly the light returned to Oma's eyes, but she shook her head and strained to speak.

"Nein...nein...nein..." was the only word she could manage. As Sabine leaned closer to hear, her grandmother's grip tightened.

"No-no-no what, Oma?"

Oma resorted to sign language, and it seemed to take every last bit of the old woman's strength to point to herself.

"Es...tut...mir...leid...," she said, wrestling horribly with each word.

"You're sorry?" Sabine wasn't sure she'd heard her grandmother right. But she looked back at Willi, and he nodded. "You don't need to be sorry for anything."

Oma shook her head with an effort that made her moan.

Sabine thought she muttered, "Your father—" But it might have been something else. She couldn't tell for sure.

The older woman in the next bed suddenly began ringing her little bell, a signal for the nurse to come quickly. That only made Oma moan again. Sabine squeezed her hand to comfort her.

"What's going on here?" a nurse in an overstarched skirt demanded as she scurried into the room. "Who are you children, and what are you doing in here?"

"They're killing her!" screamed the woman in the next bed. "They're Stasi agents, and they're going to strangle her in her bed!"

Sabine rolled her eyes.

"We're not killing anyone." She moved closer to her grandmother, as if to shield her. "We're just visiting with my oma."

"Well, you're just *done* visiting," snapped the nurse. Sabine didn't recognize her. "I will not have you disturbing the patients."

"She's not disturbing anything," Willi said, coming to Sabine's rescue. "Her brother works here. And she's just—"

The nurse whirled to glare at him. Then she brought her attention back to Sabine, roughly helping her to her feet.

"I'm sorry, young lady. Out. Now. We do not allow exceptions to visitation hours."

But Oma would not let go of Sabine's hand. She clung to her granddaughter as if for life. The nurse struggled to separate them, and Sabine could not help crying out.

"Bible, Sabine." Oma's words came clearer now. "Read...the...Bible."

At last, Oma let go, and Sabine let the nurse propel her out of the room while she puzzled over Oma's words. Of course she would read her Bible. Willi quietly followed, and Sabine couldn't help looking back at her grandmother, couldn't help wondering if she would ever see Oma again. In heaven, yes, but until then—

Oma had leaned her head back on the pillow and closed her eyes, looking much as she had when they'd first arrived. Once again, she had become that other old woman, that dying woman. Not Oma. And as the nurse escorted them toward the exit, Sabine thought she heard her oma cry: "So, so sorry. Oh, my Savior, sorry!"

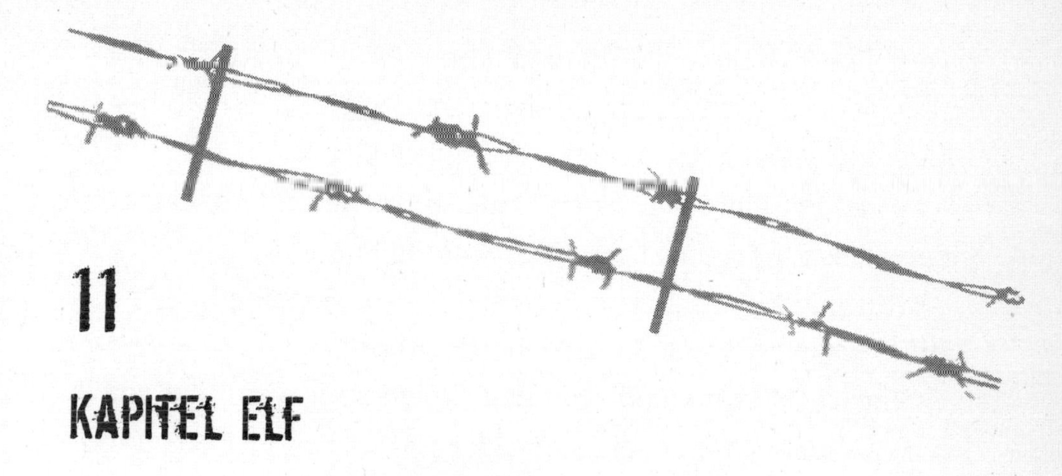

11

KAPITEL ELF

TRUSTING GRETA

"I don't understand what just happened in there." Willi scratched his head as he stood with Sabine on the front steps of St. Ludwig's.

First the mystery message from Erich's friend, then the heartbreaking apology from Oma. What did the girl want to talk to them about, and what was Oma so sorry for? And finally their quick exit, thanks to that rude nurse. Sabine crossed her arms and looked at the ornate front door, wondering.

Especially about Oma.

The door flew open. "*There* you are!" Greta exclaimed. "I was afraid you'd already left!"

She stopped next to them and caught her breath.

"Oh, well, no, we—" Sabine wasn't sure how much she should tell this girl, even though she'd said she was Erich's friend. What if she worked for the Stasi as an informant, a snitch, like half the city? She could be pretending, looking for information to get Erich in trouble. Greta seemed to read her mind and rested a hand on the girl's shoulder.

"You don't have to worry, Sabine. If we weren't on your side, believe me, you'd have been rounded up long ago."

"You said before that you wanted to ask us something?" Sabine wasn't going to believe just anything.

"Right." Greta nodded. "But first I need your word that you'll keep this just between us." The older girl looked first at Sabine, then Willi. And Sabine gave her friend a warning look, though she couldn't say it out loud: *Don't you dare mention anything about "on your honor as a Junge Pioniere."*

He held up his hand and opened his mouth, but Sabine beat him to it.

"Fine."

Whoops. What had she just promised?

Greta nodded seriously. "All right, then. We need to know about the underground...the *hole* you fell into."

"Oh, you want to know about *that*?" Willi perked up. "I've been down there. It's dark and musty, actually. And the car isn't as nice as she made me believe at first, and—"

"Willi!" Sabine interrupted. "She doesn't need to know all that."

"A car?" Greta's eyebrows registered her surprise. "Actually, all we want to know is how you managed to get down there again. By the time we figured out that's where you printed your flyers, the workers had already sealed up the street. You know of another way?"

Sabine bit her lip. "Why do you want to know?"

This time, Greta looked nervous, and she checked the door behind them. Did she really trust them or not?

"We're planning to dig a tunnel under the wall," she finally whispered. "But we need a place to start from and someplace to pile all the dirt. We want you to show us the hole because it might be the perfect place to start digging."

"Oh!" Sabine could hardly believe Greta's words. "I've heard stories about people escaping that way. I just didn't know if they were true."

"They're true. And we're going to do it too."

"But through the sewers and such. That's what they're trying now, isn't it?"

"A few have tried. But the Stasi have begun welding the manhole covers shut. Three of our friends died down there before—"

She wiped a tear with the sleeve of her blouse.

"This isn't a sewer, though," Sabine said, trying not to imagine Greta's friends in the sewer. She took a breath and explained about the underground rooms, the passageways, the way down through the bombed-out building. Greta nodded as if she were taking notes.

When Greta asked her to take them into the bunker, Sabine hesitated. Finally she said, "I guess I can. But...what about Erich?"

"Well—" Greta looked away as she straightened the little white nurse's hat pinned to her hair. "He doesn't like getting you involved, but he'll get over it."

"Yes, but is he planning to—" When Sabine closed her eyes, all she could see was the Stasi agents putting the seal on Frau Finkenkrug's door, going from apartment to apartment. Next time, it might be their mother. "Is he planning to escape too?"

The question hung in the air, and Greta swallowed hard.

"You'll have to ask him yourself. But look, I have to get back to work. Thanks for helping."

And without another word, the nurse's aide turned to go.

"Wait!" Sabine held up her hand. "Do you want me to meet you somewhere? You didn't tell me."

Greta paused in the doorway without turning around.

"Erich will let you know when it's time."

Which turned out to be sooner than Sabine expected. As in, that night just after dinner.

"I'm going for a walk." Erich rose from the table first. As usual, Uncle Heinz was just reaching for a second helping. "May I be excused?"

Uncle Heinz lifted his eyebrows at his nephew and kept chewing as he spoke. "I'm just curious; you're not spending time with anyone special at the hospital, are you?"

Erich stiffened, and Sabine nearly choked on her last bite.

"Would it be a problem if I were?" asked Erich.

Uncle Heinz stretched, making his chair creak and groan. "Maybe. I hear some of the staff there are, uh, under observation."

"You mean being watched by the Stasi? The way they've been watching me, stopping me, asking me dumb questions all the time? Every time I go out the door, old Wolfgang reports back to them!"

"I would be more careful, if I were you," Uncle Heinz warned. He frowned and kept eating while Erich went on—hotter than ever.

"What kind of a country is this? First it built a wall to keep its own people in. Then it expects everyone to spy on each other to keep people from disagreeing with it?"

Aunt Gertrud closed her eyes as if she felt another headache coming on.

"Erich." Their mother turned pale. "Let's not talk politics at the table. Please."

Uncle Heinz tossed his fork to the table and pushed back.

"I'm just telling him that he needs to be careful who he talks to, that's all. The Stasi are only trying to do their jobs. And I'm trying to do Erich a favor."

"Thanks, Onkel Heinz." Erich leaned over to dip his hands in the bowl of sudsy water in the sink. "I'll keep that in mind."

Case closed—for now. A few moments later, Erich brushed by Sabine in the hallway.

"Follow me in ten minutes," he whispered.

Nine minutes later, she was standing on the street in the early summer evening, wondering what her big brother was up to. It didn't surprise her when he stepped out from behind Fegelein's *Bäckerei.*

"All right, now listen"—he leveled a finger at her in a big-brotherly way—"I didn't want to bring you into this, and I told them so. But we couldn't see a better way. So all you're going to do," he continued, "is show us the way in, and we'll take it from there."

"Nein." She kept going. "I told Mama I'm going to check up on Willi. So that's what I'm going to do first."

"But I told them we'd meet them in—"

"I'm not going to lie to Mama. Besides, Willi's in on this too."

Erich grumbled something about how they might as well show Wolfgang a big sign announcing their plan to build an escape tunnel. She did her best to ignore him, and a half hour later, three of them approached the bombed-out apartment building.

"We're not just all going to march right in, are we?" Willi looked around nervously. The streets were still full of people at 7:00 p.m. on a warm summer evening.

"And what about your friends?" asked Sabine.

"You just show me which part of the building." Erich ignored their questions. "Keep walking, tell me in a low voice, and don't point."

Okay. She could do this.

"About in the middle, past those two walls that fell on each other, around the back side and—"

"Good enough," he said, interrupting her. "Stop behind that pile of broken bricks, then go in first. I'll follow when nobody else is walking by. By the way, how'd you ever get in there from this direction without anybody seeing you?"

"I don't know." Sabine shrugged. "I guess I was just careful about it. And the first time, as you know, I sort of fell into it."

Another groan from her brother. But Sabine did as he'd said, climbing carefully through the rubble until she stood once again in the room with the crumbled walls and the flowery wallpaper.

Not bad for a girl on crutches! She congratulated herself as she looked around. What had this room once been? A living room? An office? Hard to tell. With all the walls tumbled upon one another, it looked like the inside of an earthquake site.

"You're sure this is it?" her brother asked when he joined her a couple of minutes later.

Then two others seemed to melt out of the shadows: Greta and Dietrich.

"Whoa." Willi whistled as he joined them, not as quiet. "You guys really must be serious about this. Wait until I show you the car."

"Where is it?" asked Dietrich. Sabine knew he meant the trapdoor, not the car. She pointed to his feet. He stood on a low pile of crumbled cement blocks.

"You're kidding." He lifted first one foot, then the other. "We would never have found this on our own."

"We covered it back up with junk last time." She got down on her knees and started to brush away the rubble. "Here, let me show you."

"You don't need to do that." Erich put his hand on her shoulder. "All we needed was for you to show us the place. We can take it from here."

But Sabine didn't stop.

"If you're building a tunnel, we're going to help."

She glanced at Willi out of the corner of her eye to see him nod. Erich only laughed.

"What are you talking about? You're going home before Onkel Heinz reports you to Comrade Ulbricht. And you can't go home all dirty again."

"What about you?"

"That's not the question. Besides, this is going to be dangerous, you know."

"I know. That's why you need my help."

"You're crazy. And you can't just leave Mutti here in Berlin with Oma."

"But you can?"

"Listen, I'm helping my friends. That's different."

"I say it's not."

"And I say you need to go home before you get hurt."

"I'm not a little kid. I'm thirteen, you know."

"Doesn't matter. I say no."

Sabine wasn't surprised. But Dietrich looked over at Greta, who nodded.

"They already know where the entrance is," Dietrich told Erich quietly. "And we could use the help, Erich."

"What are you talking about?" Erich's voice rose a few notches. "She's my sister, and I say she goes home."

But it looked as if Dietrich could be just as stubborn. Or rather, Dietrich and Greta. Two against one.

"You remember how we agreed to do things," she said. "Dietrich leads."

"But if we disagree—" Erich wasn't giving up just yet.

"If we disagree, the three of us vote."

Sabine looked from her brother to the others.

"They can stay, if they want," Greta finally announced. "As long as they keep quiet about what we're doing."

Willi zipped a finger across his lips and grinned. But when Sabine had a chance to think for a second, she wasn't so sure. Not about keeping quiet. But as she looked down at the hole they'd opened in the floor, she wondered: what had they gotten themselves into?

12

KAPITEL ZWÖLF

TUNNEL FELLOWSHIP

"All right, everybody, listen up." The flickering candle behind Dietrich cast a weird monster shadow on the opposite wall of the bunker. Sabine and Willi sat on the back end of their car, watching. Four, five, six... Sabine wondered if they were all from the hospital, and if they could all keep the secret. And the older guys—all about Erich's age or a little younger—glanced over at Willi and Sabine with looks that said, *What are* they *doing here?*

"I'm glad you're all here," Dietrich continued. "Anton and Albricht—"

Sabine looked twice when a candle flicker illuminated the two faces. Unless she was mistaken—

"And yes, Sabine, they're twins."

Sabine nodded, and Willi chuckled.

"I noticed," she told them. "Only, is there any way to tell you apart?"

Anton grinned and flexed an impressive set of arms. "I'm the better-looking one."

"You always say that." Albricht jabbed his brother with an elbow. They could have been a wrestling team, with square shoulders and big chests. "But the only way to tell us apart is the scar."

He leaned close to the candle he was holding and pointed to his jaw.

"There. See? Ouch!"

A little *too* close to the candle.

"Albricht, scar; Anton, no scar," he finished, rubbing his chin.

Sabine smiled and nodded. "Okay. Great. Don't burn yourself too."

The others laughed while the third newcomer kept looking over his shoulder, over his head, down at his shoes. He took off his glasses, put them back on—

"And everyone knows Gerhard, right?" Dietrich made the introduction. "He works in the linen room."

Gerhard nodded but narrowed his eyes at Sabine and Willi.

"No one told me there would be little kids," he began, giving his head a good scratch.

"We're not little kids." Sabine stood up to the challenge. "And we found this bunker in the first place."

"Hmm." Gerhard crossed his arms.

"She's my sister," announced Erich. "She's... okay."

Sabine relaxed when her brother defended her to the group.

"So now that we have that settled," Dietrich went on, "let's lay down the rules of the Tunnel Fellowship and what we're going to do."

Greta brought out a handful of cold candle stubs, giving one to each of them.

"We're going to need to depend on one another down here," Dietrich told them, his voice growing more serious. "Even for our lives, maybe. So now's your chance to leave."

No one moved.

"We dig together. We escape together. No one is left behind."

Sabine didn't dare look at her older brother. Did that include their mother and Oma? What about Willi's family? Dietrich lit Greta's candle with his.

"We pledge to one another that we will never reveal this place, this plan, or this fellowship to anyone outside this room."

Greta turned to light Erich's candle.

"And if any of us has to drop out of the fellowship, we still pledge to keep the secrets—all the secrets."

Erich turned to light Albricht's candle—or maybe it was Anton's. And so Dietrich went on about always coming to the entrance alone, making sure no one discovered the bunker, where they would pile the dirt, how they would keep watch. His words echoed through the underground rooms until they all stood facing one another, flaming candle stubs in hand.

"We're all agreed, then?" asked Dietrich.

"Ja." Greta nodded. Each, in turn, promised as they went around the circle.

At his turn, Willi nodded solemnly. *"Ja*...ouch!" he cried, sending his candle stub flying. He shook his hand wildly. "Hot wax! Right on my hand."

Everyone burst out laughing, even Dietrich—for a moment. Then he brought them back to business.

"All right, then, let's get to it. The twins will be our main diggers, and Gerhard and I will give them breaks when we can. Erich is our engineer and safety man, and Greta will make sure we're tunneling in the right direction."

"What about us?" Willi wanted to know.

"Oh, right." Dietrich held up his finger. "One of you is going to help dump dirt away from the tunnel, and the other is going to watch the entry."

Willi nodded.

"And in a few weeks—" Dietrich looked at them, and Sabine felt a stab of excitement. Yes, in a few weeks. If no one saw them coming and going. If no one leaked the secret. If no one discovered what they were doing. If, if, if—

Her excitement exploded into fear. Everyone froze as they heard someone moving in the ruined building above them.

"Shh!" Erich snuffed his candle first. A moment later, the darkness wrapped around them like a cold blanket, and Sabine shivered at the sound of someone scratching at the trapdoor. Willi grabbed her arm. "What...was...*that*?" he whispered in her ear. For a minute, she thought he was going to climb up on her shoulders. She didn't answer, just peeled off his fingers and headed for the bottom of the spiral stairway.

"Sabine?" Her brother could not have known it was her climbing the stairs, praying they would hold her one more time. But she had to get to the top before it was too late. She could see the weak light filtering through the cracks. And she could hear the whimpering and scratching—and she knew her guess had been right. Using her crutch for balance, she dug her shoulder up and into the door, popping it open.

"Woof!"

"Hey!" Erich cried from below, and Sabine felt the stairway groan and creak, as if it would give way any moment. She held on to the floor above her, just in case, while Bismarck happily cleaned her face and motored his tail in eggbeater circles.

"Easy." She did her best to wiggle away, but Bismarck kept right on her. Meanwhile, everyone below wanted to know what was going on—as if she alone could see the enemy through the submarine's periscope.

"What's up there?"

"What is she doing?"

"Close the door!"

"Get her *down*!"

Voices boiled and blended into full-scale panic, until Sabine felt a pair of hands grab her ankles. She had to grab something too, to keep her balance, and when her hands missed the edge of the opening, she connected with Bismarck's two front legs.

Off balance, she felt the mound of moving dog fur fall on top of her, while strong arms wrapped around her waist and eased her toward the floor.

"Wow. You're heavier than I thought!"

That's when all three of them tumbled backward. Erich probably took the worst of it; Sabine had her brother-cushion behind and the dog-cushion in front. Bismarck yelped in surprise (Sabine didn't blame him) while the door above their heads slammed shut once more and darkness reclaimed the bunker.

"I'm okay." Sabine had lost one of her crutches, though.

"Glad to hear it." Erich groaned. "But did we just drag down what I think we just dragged down?"

That only jump-started the Tunnel Fellowship panic squad again:

"Did you bring something down here?"

"I'm getting out."

"Did somebody follow us?"

"What's going *on*?"

Finally Dietrich brought a match to life, and the pool of light seemed to quiet everyone. Bismarck stared at him with his tongue-wagging happy face.

"*That's* what caused all this commotion?" asked Erich.

"He was just trying to find us," Willi said, defending Bismarck. He scratched the dog behind the ears. "Good boy."

"Your dog?" Dietrich asked as he relit a couple of candles.

"He seems to think so, but no."

"What if someone followed him here?" Count on Gerhard for the dark side. "We need to get rid of him, now."

"No!" Sabine and Willi both shielded their adopted pet.

"Gerhard has a point," Dietrich agreed. "He could give us away."

"He'll work for us." Sabine tried to think fast. "He can be a guard dog, or pull a cart, or—"

Erich shook his head and stared at the floor, thinking.

"I'll probably regret this," Dietrich said, taking his candle and heading for the far rooms. "But he can stay—for now. If he makes any noise or gets into any other trouble, though, that's it. No second chances."

Sabine nodded seriously and reached for her dropped crutch, but Bismarck had already beaten her to it. Taking one of the handles in his mouth, he wagged his tail and dragged it closer.

"See?" she told them. "He's already helping out. And he's really gentle."

"He is kind of cute," Greta admitted, holding her hand out to the dog. "Floppy ears means he's not all shepherd, though, right?"

As Sabine nodded, the hair on the back of Bismarck's neck stood up, and he gave a low, throaty growl. Greta gasped and pulled her hand back.

"What—," she began.

But Bismarck had pointed his attention back toward the hole the street workers had opened—where Sabine had fallen.

"That's it," muttered Gerhard. "I'm not working down here with a growling beast—"

"Shh!" Sabine interrupted. She hugged Bismarck tightly. The dog quieted as well, though he kept alert.

In the silence, they could all faintly hear a worker in the distance.

"I think it's somebody working on a pipe up there," Erich told them.

"Did anybody else hear that?" asked Sabine. When they all shook their heads no, she continued, "See? If we have Bismarck around, he can hear things we can't. And he wasn't growling at Greta. He was just protecting us."

Of course that seemed like a good thing to Sabine, even as they worked their way back out a half hour later. Willi and Sabine stood with Bismarck for a minute on the street.

"That's where we're going to end up, right?" Willi pointed at the small church cemetery on the other side of Bernauerstrasse, on the other side of the wall—the other side of the world.

"Just forty-two feet of digging." Sabine quietly echoed her big brother's words. He was the project engineer, after all; he and Greta would figure out how to come up in the right place, not in the middle of one of the graves. But what if they didn't measure right? She shivered.

"Back away!" The Vopo guard's harsh command made Sabine jump as the guard pushed his way between them and the fence. She saw him finger the trigger of a wicked-looking weapon and quickly grabbed Bismarck by the collar to stop his growl.

"Sorry. I didn't realize we were too close." Sabine did her best to backpedal, but she caught the tip of one crutch on her heel and almost fell.

The soldier's face softened as he pushed the helmet back off his forehead. "You need to find another place to walk your dog," he told them, and he bent down to pat Bismarck, who'd quieted. "A person could get hurt on this fence."

"We were just on our way home," Willi told him, but his voice cracked.

"Well, your mother's going to be upset with you." The soldier bent a little closer. "How did you get so dirty? Digging a garden or something?"

Uh-oh. Sabine looked down at the grime on her pant legs. Sure enough. Bismarck's paws looked just as filthy.

"Uh, it's the dog," she said, thinking quickly. "He likes to, um, roll in the dirt, and he always gets me dirty."

The man studied them closely.

"Well, I'd clean up a bit before I got home, if I were you." And he waved them off with the end of his gun. "Go on now."

They didn't wait for another invitation.

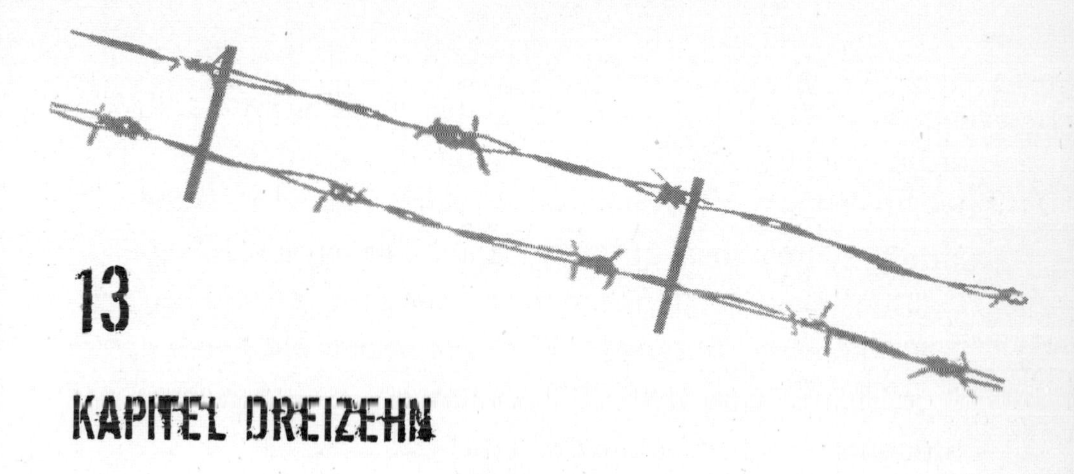

13

KAPITEL DREIZEHN

SIGHTED

"Day Two of the Tunnel Fellowship—" Willi held his school notebook nearly pressed to his face, his pencil nearly poking him in the glasses. "Digging begins under Bernauerstrasse."

"I don't understand how you can write like that," Sabine told him. She finished off the last chunk of French bread she'd brought along as a mid-afternoon snack.

"You get used to it."

"And besides, I don't think it's a good idea to write about what we're doing. What if someone finds it, like your father?"

Willi flipped the page around to show her. "Does that answer your question?" he asked.

"Looks more like Chinese than German," she answered as she peered at the horrible chicken scratching of tiny letters.

"It's backward, skip a word, and... well, that's the secret part of the code."

"Hmm." She hadn't expected that from Willi, but then Willi kept surprising her. So he kept writing, checking back and forth between his notes and his compass. Sabine returned to the little telescope they'd set up in Willi's window, near the curtain, so they could quickly hide it if anybody looked up.

"Don't move it. I think I found a good spot," he told her.

"All I see are gravestones over there. That is *not* a good spot."

No matter what, she would *not* tunnel up through a casket, through a dead body. *Nein. Durchaus nicht!* No way!

"I mean closer to the church building. There's a little spot of grass, I think. You tell me."

Sabine squinted through the eyepiece. "Okay, I see it," she told him. "There's a bench, then a patch of grass, then the building. I don't know if anyone can see it from the street."

"Perfect. We'll tell your brother?"

"I guess so. I don't know if he'll listen to us, though. We are just the lowly dirt carriers."

Willi shrugged. "I don't mind. I guess I've learned to be content with whatever's going on around me."

"That sounds like something from the Bible, not you."

"Hey." He grinned. "You caught that."

"Yeah. But are you content enough to stay on this side of the wall for the rest of your life?"

Willi didn't answer right away. When he did, his voice sounded softer. "My mom wants us to leave, really badly. Even lying there in the hospital, that's all she ever talks about. For her children, she says. She makes Papa crazy."

"But she's getting better, right?"

"Well, the baby is still tiny, but she's healthy. The doctor said they can come home in a few days."

"That's great. What about your dad, though? Why is he so—"

"Papa...Papa is, uh...Look, Sabine, I don't really want to talk about it."

"But we have to talk about it. What if we dig the tunnel, and they won't come?"

"I know, I know. But you should see Papa every time he hears about someone escaping."

"Not like Onkel Heinz?"

"No, no. He hates it here, but he acts like...like they died of a horrible disease, and we can't talk about it, or else we'll catch the disease too."

"So what happens if you try to say anything?" she asked.

"I can't...I'm not like you, Sabine. You don't care what other people think. Me, I—"

Willi's voice trailed off, and Sabine looked over at her friend. His thick lenses made his eyes look way too big for his face, sort of like fish eyes. He took off the glasses and wiped them on his shirt. She wished she knew what to say to him.

"Don't worry about your family," she finally managed. "We'll figure something out."

"Hope you're right." But he couldn't know that a scared little girl hid behind all her big talk and big promises. She just put the telescope back to her eye. Looking busy and in charge was the best way to not look afraid.

Down on the street, she could actually see the tight curls, tucked beneath a somber gray hairnet, on a passing woman's head. "This is kind of fun," she told him. "I can see—"

The scowl of a very irritated Vopo guard, looking straight at her, filled the view of the telescope.

"Uh-oh." Sabine ducked. "Not so good."

"What?" Willi obviously had no idea what she had just seen.

She pulled the curtain shut. "We have to get rid of this telescope, quick."

"Are you kidding? My father gave me that for Christmas. It's—"

"It's going to get us in a lot of trouble if we don't hide from the Vopo who just saw me with it. *Now!*"

"Why didn't you say so?"

Willi quickly looked around and pointed under the kitchen sink. They squeezed together behind a checkered skirt that hid stuff like the scrub brushes, soap flakes, and a waste bucket.

"Have you even emptied the garbage since your mother went to the hospital?" Sabine whispered, wrinkling her nose in distaste.

"Sorry." He sneezed once, then again. "I just thought maybe no one would look here."

Maybe the Vopo would, and maybe they wouldn't. But Sabine knew she and Willi had to keep silent when the Vopo broke down the front door of the Stumpffs' apartment.

"On Day Two, Willi and Sabine find a safe place for the tunnel to end," Willi whispered, as he planned his next journal entry. "Except—"

They expected the Vopo to break in any minute to capture them. They'd be tried as spies. And Willi had just pulled out his journal again to fill it with more chicken scratching.

"Would you put that thing away?" Sabine hissed. She stiffened when she heard the sound of boots coming up the stairway.

"There!" Willi whispered. "You hear it?"

She nodded silently.

"We don't answer the door, right?" Willi asked, panicked.

Sabine just sat with her knees in her face, waiting for the man who had seen her to burst into the apartment and drag them off. Strangely, the door didn't pop off its hinges; it just squeaked open the way it always did. "Willi!" a man called, followed by a whistle.

"Oh, no." Willi rolled out of his hiding place, sending a glass vase skittering across the linoleum. "It's my dad."

Good thing Sabine managed to crawl out from under the sink before Herr Stumpff came into the kitchen.

"So you're the Sabine I've heard so much about." Herr Stumpff looked like a grown-up version of Willi, only bald and a little grease-stained. He smiled and held out his rough mechanic's hand. "Willi tells me your grandmother is in the same hospital as my wife and daughter."

"Yes, sir. Different floors, though." She wondered what to do when the Vopo pounded on the door. Herr Stumpff looked at the mess on the floor, then at her shoulder.

"Er, can I help you find something?"

"Oh—no, sir. We were just...that is—"

That's when she noticed the week-old potato peel stuck on her shoulder. "Actually— She felt her face heating up as she flicked the peel into the trash. "I was about to help Willi...get dinner started."

Which explained everything, right? Willi stooped to pick up a runaway scrub brush as his father gave them a curious look.

"That's very nice of you, Sabine. But I thought Willi and I would eat at the hospital tonight and keep his mother company. Of course, you're welcome to join us—if it's all right with your mother, that is."

"Oh." Sabine replaced another scrub brush and vase. "I should head home. But thank you for offering."

She resigned herself to being arrested in the hallway. But Herr Stumpff kept her from leaving.

"I'm sorry, Sabine, but you should know something before you go out there. You too, Willi."

Sabine nearly choked on her spit. *What did he know?*

"There's another empty apartment on the third floor. The police have sealed it off."

Oh. *Another* one.

"Do not stop there to look," he went on, "and don't ask questions. Just walk on by."

Willi's father looked dead serious as he let her go and went to the sink to wash his hands.

"In fact," he said, "just pretend it's not there and stay out of trouble."

"Yes, sir." She nodded, but her stomach knotted up. Pretend it's not there? That's exactly what was all wrong with this mixed-up country!

Pretend he's not there. And Hitler will go away.

Pretend it's not real. And the war will soon be over.

Pretend you don't notice. And the wall won't matter so much.

Pretend, pretend, pretend. And the Stasi will be nice to us.

Well, it never worked that way. But she tried her best not to glare at her friend's father, no matter how silly he sounded, as she told them good-bye and let herself out.

"Thanks again," she called back, knowing she would run straight into the guard as he made his way up the stairs.

But the fifth floor looked deserted, just like the fourth and third floors. Oh, and she caught a glimpse of the empty apartment, the one that wasn't really there. And though she hadn't known the people who had lived there, she prayed for them.

On the second floor, a couple of stooped men marched home, never looking up from the worn carpet runner. So she worked her way down the last few steps to the street level, one at a time, the same way she always did—but holding her breath, ready to flee. As if a girl with crutches could have outrun a soldier with a gun.

Sabine carefully pushed the outside door open and looked up and down the street.

No Stasi. Not even any Vopos.

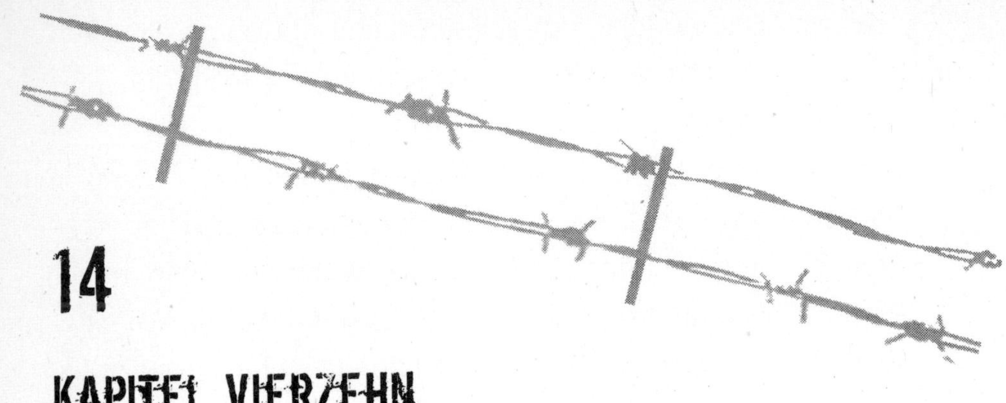

14

KAPITEL VIERZEHN

PANIC ATTACK

Sabine stumbled through the chamber with her wooden buckets full of dirt and grunted as she passed by Willi going the other way. Carrying buckets with crutches was quite a trick, but she managed by hanging them on both ends of a makeshift yoke—a stout board—balanced on her shoulders.

And no, she wasn't going to let anyone tell her she couldn't do such a thing. Willi knew better than to even mention it.

"One hundred forty-two," she told him.

"And that's just today."

Right. By the end of the first week, it was getting harder and harder to find room in the underground garage for more tunnel dirt. Even with all the rooms! She paused for just a minute to catch her breath.

"You're lucky," she whispered to Bismarck, who sat and watched them from his favorite spot on the front seat of the

Volkswagen. "You don't have to drag all this dirt out. But then, I asked to help, right? So who's complaining?"

Bismarck stopped chewing his bone to look up at her, his head tilted sideways. The nagging little signal bell on the car's windshield frame tinkled once. They'd tied one end of a kite string to it and rolled the string into the tunnel, where Anton and Albricht dug away for several hours at a time. One ring meant "Come and get more dirt." She forgot what two bells meant. But three bells meant "Help!"

"Coming, coming!" Sabine picked up her buckets again, closed her eyes, and headed in. Good thing she'd worked through her claustro-whatever. Fear of dark closets and closed-in dark places. Or dark, damp places like tunnels, where the sides could collapse and bury you alive. *What would Mother think if I didn't come home to dinner?* Already she'd used just about every excuse she could think of, trying her best not to lie to Mama. But how did her clothes get so dirty, even when she made an effort to stay clean by changing into scrubs from the hospital?

And, heavens, look at those fingernails! *Du lieber Himmel,* they'd gotten so dark and dirty. And the candles Erich placed on little stands every few feet don't really help, either, since the tunnel was hardly wide enough to crawl through or turn around in, and the sides brushed against you as if they were alive, grabbing, clawing at you, squeezing the breath out of you—

"Sabine?"

She opened her eyes. Erich stood staring at her in the candlelight, his hand on her shoulder. She blinked her eyes and tried to remember. Had he just said something, or had he just sneaked up on her for fun? And how did she get back in the main room?

"What's wrong, Sabine? Why are you ringing the bell out here? Are you hurt?"

Well, of course not. But that didn't explain her sobbing and shaking. Greta and Willi had come running at the sound of the bells, while Bismarck tried to lick her face.

"Sabine?" Greta took her wrist, the way a doctor would have done. "Sabine, relax. Slow down. Your heart is racing."

And her head wouldn't stop spinning.

"I don't know—" Sabine tried to explain, but nothing came out. She saw herself back inside the closet at the hospital, and she knew Nurse Ilse would keep the door locked until she stopped crying. But she also knew how to stop.

"I'll be good," she whispered. "I promise."

"I'm taking you home," announced Erich. And by the tone of his voice, she knew better than to argue. She let him lead her to the trapdoor.

When they reached the street, she made Erich stop while she waited for the tightness in her chest to settle down, for the crawly feeling on her skin to go away. She took a deep breath as a Trabi sputtered by, and the car's nose-curdling fumes made her choke. At least the afternoon sun felt good on her face.

"I don't know if you should go down there again," Erich said quietly.

What are you talking about? And who do you think you are, some kind of doctor? Just because you work in a hospital— Sabine's mind screamed.

Sabine swallowed the bitter taste in her mouth, sniffed, and wiped away the tears with her sleeve. There. Enough baby-bawling. She set her jaw, adjusted her crutches, and shrugged her brother's hand away.

"Thanks for your help," she told him as she headed down Bernauerstrasse on her own power. She navigated around a tree, full in its summer umbrella of leaves. And she *did* appreciate his help, except— "I can make it from here. But I'll be back tomorrow."

So he let her go, and a few minutes later, she stopped at the faucet in the alleyway beside their apartment building. If she looked up, she could probably see her mother through the living room window, just above her head. Instead, she spent a few minutes cleaning up in the cool water. She hoped she'd rinsed away the tracks of her tears—and the mud. The sound of footsteps made her turn.

"Glad you made it back home." Erich stepped up to the faucet and began to wash up himself. Sabine rested on her crutches, glaring at him.

"Told you I would. Why'd you follow? Didn't you believe me?"

"You can be pretty stubborn sometimes. I just wanted to make sure."

"Fine. But I'm still going back tomorrow. You can't talk me out of it."

He didn't answer, just scrubbed his hands like a surgeon, over and over.

"Did you hear me?" she tried again.

"I heard you. I'm just going to have to talk with Greta and Dietrich. I don't think it's a good idea. Especially not after today."

"What do you want me to do, stay home all day where it's safe, the way Mama wants me to?"

"Don't bring her into it," Erich snapped back. "If it wasn't for Mama—"

"I know, I know. I'm sorry. I just don't want to end up like all our neighbors."

"Not *all* of them, Sabine."

"No? The only ones who have any guts have already escaped. And then everyone else tiptoes by the sealed apartments, like they're not allowed to look. It makes me sick, Erich."

"I know how you feel, Sabine. And I'm helping my friends because they need me. But maybe, sometimes, God calls us to stay."

"Not me. Every time I look across that fence, I know where I'm supposed to be. Free. Over there."

"Then what about our family, Sabine? Or is this just for you?"

Low blow. She fought hard to stop her angry tears. And she gripped the handles of her crutches, wishing she could use them to knock her big brother across the side of his head.

"That's not fair."

"Why not?"

"Because this is finally something I can *do*, something that will actually make a difference. Not just passing out stupid flyers or trying to get people to strike. But you've decided to swoop in and say it's 'too dangerous.'"

She didn't mean to sound quite as sassy as she probably did. But Erich didn't miss a beat.

"I'm just thinking about what's best for you and what's best for our family. Maybe you haven't thought of it that way yet. But I have."

"Well, then, tell me something: why are you mixed up in this?"

"I told you. They're my friends, Sabine. I want to help them. I *have* to help them."

"Yeah, but are you going too, or not?"

Erich studied his shoes and pressed his lips together. He did that when he got upset. But Sabine didn't care. She had to know.

"So will you go with your hospital buddies, or stay?"

"Keep your voice down, all right?" Erich hissed.

"All right." She lowered her voice a notch or two. "But you always told me God put you in the hospital for a reason. Right here in East Berlin. Did he, or didn't he?"

Again Erich didn't answer right away. Was it all boys, or just Erich that had to think so long before responding? Sometimes it almost made her want to strangle him. She looked straight at Erich, waiting.

"I've asked myself the same thing, Sabine."

"And?"

"And I don't know, for sure."

"Well, thanks for nothing." She turned away.

"I never said I had all the answers."

And then he burped, just like Uncle Heinz, like a bullfrog. Why did boys always have to do that? Disgusting.

"Excuse you," she told him, glancing back over her shoulder with a frown.

"That wasn't me." He put out his hands and looked up, and her stomach flipped. Just above their heads, the breeze caught a corner of her mother's lacy window curtain. When had Uncle Heinz opened the window?

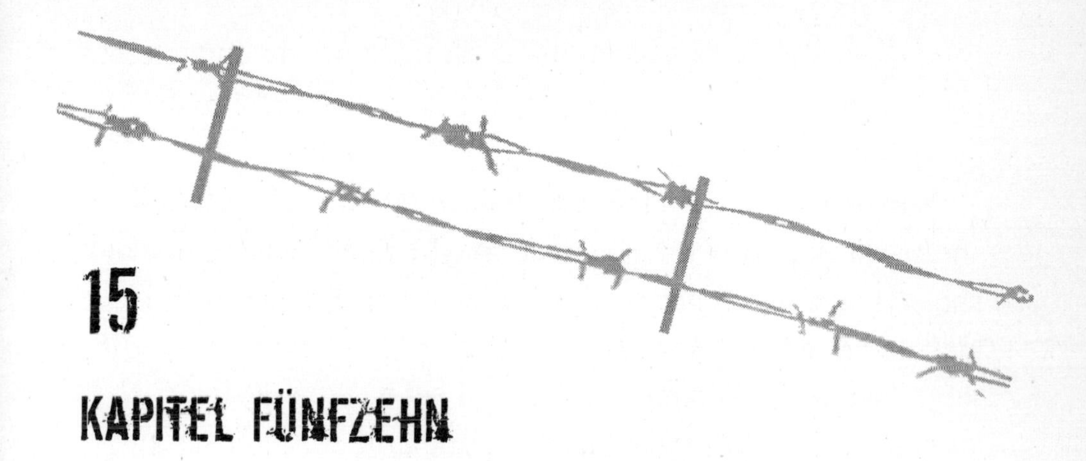

15

KAPITEL FÜNFZEHN

HOMECOMING

"Your mama and the baby finally get to come home? How exciting." Sabine did her best to keep up with her friend as they walked to St. Ludwig's. "After a whole month in the hospital!"

"Five weeks. And sure I'm excited." He squinted both ways at the corner of Invalidenstrasse. Sabine grabbed his sleeve just in time to keep him from stepping into the path of a speeding Trabi. "I'm just not sure anybody's going to get any sleep at home anymore. Have you heard that kid scream since they brought her out of intensive care?"

"I've heard." Sabine smiled as they crossed the street. Not that she had any idea how having a new baby sister would change things. Sabine couldn't wait to see them "graduate" from the maternity ward.

"Do you think they'll let me hold little Effi?" she asked. "She's about the cutest baby I've ever seen."

"I don't know. They've pretty much had Elfriede under lights for the past few weeks. Remember? Like a little plant in a greenhouse."

Sabine laughed. And for one happy moment, she wished she could skip through the street, maybe dance a little. Instead, she swung high on her crutches. Watch out! She could still kick up her heels...sort of.

"What are you *doing*?" Willi didn't get it. "You're crazy."

"Maybe," she answered as he opened the hospital's front door. A nurse wheeled Frau Stumpff toward them, baby bundled in her arms. Good timing! Herr Stumpff kept pace alongside.

"She's beautiful," Sabine cooed when the wheelchair came near. Yellow mottled skin, button nose, bright little blue eyes, little curly tufts of dark hair— "And so tiny. Like a little baby doll."

Sabine offered her pinky to Effi and laughed when the baby's miniature fingers curled around it. After all the little one had gone through, Sabine did her best not to breathe on the baby. Willi's mother smiled weakly as she watched her daughter. Herr Stumpff walked away for a moment to sign some papers at the front desk.

"It will be good to get home, won't it?" his mother asked. "I hear Sabine's taught you to cook since I've been in the hospital."

Willi sort of coughed. Well...if you called burned boiled oatmeal *cooking*.

"Willi, could you do me a favor?" Herr Stumpff looked up from the paperwork. "We left your mother's suitcase in her room. Could you—"

"Sure." Willi nodded and hurried away. And since Sabine knew she couldn't help much, she decided to check in with Greta and Dietrich. Erich wouldn't report to work for another couple of hours.

"I'll be right back." She stroked the baby's cheek before following Willi. But by the time she'd reached Greta's second-floor duty station, Willi had already picked up his mother's suitcase and beaten her there.

"You're sure she's not working today?" she heard Willi ask. He looked puzzled. "She always works Mondays."

But Frau Ziegler, the supervising nurse, didn't even look up. She just chewed on the end of her pencil and flipped open a notebook. Sabine noticed the woman's knuckles had turned white, gripping the edge of the desk.

Odd. She'd always had a smile for them.

"What about Dietrich?" Sabine wondered as she neared the counter.

"Dietrich no longer works here, either."

Either? Finally the nurse looked up at them. The dark panic in her eyes nearly made Sabine's heart stop. "Please. I must ask you to leave right away. This is not a good time for you to be here."

Wait—what had happened to Greta and Dietrich? The shock must have registered on their faces, but Frau Ziegler only snapped her pencil in half as her face turned pink, and she pointed to the exit. Her eyes, however, looked in the opposite direction. How strange. As if she were pointing at something they should know about, something she couldn't tell them about.

"Please go," she hissed. "Or they'll arrest you too. Go now, and don't come back."

But they didn't move quickly enough. A dark-haired man in a starched shirt emerged from a storeroom down the hall—the direction Frau Ziegler had pointed with her eyes. He held several large folders stuffed with papers. An older-looking nurse with her own armload of folders matched him step for step as they came down the hall, deep in conversation.

Sabine had never seen the woman before, but she looked like some kind of supervisor. They heard her say that she would do everything she could to help out the government. And that it served those two interns right for thinking they could get away with something so outrageous. The dark-haired man thanked her and said she'd been extremely helpful, and if she suspected any others—

A chill ran up Sabine's spine; she knew at a glance everything she needed to know about the man.

A Stasi *agent!*

With wide eyes and a quick nod of thanks to Frau Ziegler, Willi and Sabine turned away and hurried as fast as Sabine's crutches would allow them. Greta and Dietrich—arrested! Sabine and Willi had to warn the others, now! Anton and

Albricht worked in the cafeteria; Gerhard collected linens from all over the hospital. But Sabine had no idea whether they were working today, or in the tunnel.

Erich would know.

"Oh, great." Willi stopped short at the top of a flight of stairs. "I left Mama's suitcase at the desk."

Sabine moaned. But what else could they do? She sat down in an empty wheelchair for a moment to think, then looked up at Willi.

"Push me back there," she told him. "I look more like a patient here than you do."

"But all the nurses know us."

"Not the one with the Stasi agent. And I don't think they saw our faces. They'll just think I'm another cripple, out for some fresh air."

Willi rolled his eyes and planted his hands on his hips. "I don't know how I let you talk me into your plans."

"You're the one who forgot the suitcase, not me."

Willi couldn't argue with that, so he pushed Sabine back toward the nursing station. Frau Ziegler looked up in alarm, but the agent and his nurse didn't seem to notice them as they rolled up.

"*Um Verzeihung bitte.*" Sabine cleared her throat and tapped the man's leg with her crutch. "Excuse me, please?"

"Oh. *Ja?*" He glanced up from his papers.

"Would you please hand me my case?" Sabine smiled and pointed at the floor next to him. As he bent to pick it up, she gripped the armrests of the wheelchair to keep her hands from shaking out of control.

"*Danke schön.*" She smiled sweetly as she thanked him and took the suitcase from his hand. But inside she screamed: *Turn this thing around, and get us out of here!*

As if he could hear her, Willi spun her around and nearly sprinted away.

Once they'd gotten far enough to talk safely, Willi said, "I have to stay and help my mother." He waved the suitcase.

"Of course you do. But I have to find my brother before the Stasi get to him too. I hope he knows where to find the others."

Twenty minutes later, breathless, she found her brother in the hall, just leaving their apartment.

"Erich! . . . Wait. I need to talk to you."

"Sorry, Sabine, I'm late," Erich said, distracted by the time. He almost brushed by her. "Can we talk when I get off my shift, tonight after dinner?"

"No! You have to listen—right now!" She swung her crutch and nailed him in the leg to get his attention. "Please!"

"Hey, you don't have to attack me." But he stopped to listen. With each word, he looked more worried.

"You're sure the guy was Stasi?" He rubbed his chin.

"Yes. Who else would wear a jacket like that in the middle of summer?"

"And you're sure Greta and Dietrich didn't just change shifts or something?" he asked.

"I *told* you what Frau Ziegler said! They've been arrested, Erich. *Arrested.*"

"Okay." Erich's shoulders fell. "I believe you. And Ziggy's on our side. But she doesn't know what we're doing. She doesn't even know who's involved."

"Erich, you can't go back there. You'll be next."

"Maybe, maybe not. Greta and Dietrich won't tell them anything. And I need to warn the others. The only question is—"

"No, Erich, can't you see? This is serious."

The apartment door creaked open, and Uncle Heinz signaled for them to join him. How much had he heard?

"You should listen to your sister," their uncle said gravely once they'd followed him inside.

"What are you talking about?" Erich narrowed his eyes as if seeing his uncle for the first time.

"Let's not play games here." Uncle Heinz ran a hand through his hair as he paced across the room and pulled down the window shade. "I can't help you unless you cooperate."

Uncle Heinz had heard everything!

"My poor innocent nephew," Uncle Heinz sighed when Erich stayed silent. "The boy who disappears at night and comes home late with dirt under his fingernails. Wolfgang told me all about your comings and goings, and it's getting embarrassing."

The words sent chills down Sabine's spine, and she thought back to the argument she'd had with Erich in the alley. Uncle Heinz had probably heard every word they'd said then too.

Suddenly he sprang into action, grabbing Erich by the loose collar of his shirt and pulling him closer.

"Now you listen to me," he wheezed, as if it took all his breath to move so quickly. "I know you're not a loyal party member, and I know you don't pay attention to Comrade Ulbricht's speeches. I've made excuses for you, and I've looked the other way because you're my little sister's boy. I promised her once a long time ago that I'd watch out for you. And I keep my promises."

"Onkel Heinz!" Sabine reached out for her uncle's hairy arm. "Don't hurt him. Erich hasn't done anything wrong."

Uncle Heinz stared at her for a second before he laughed nervously and let Erich go.

"Nothing wrong, eh? I wish it were true. But let's talk about your pitiful choice of friends, shall we? The ones who have gotten themselves arrested? In fact, they're all in custody right now, charged with treasonous activity."

All? Treasonous activity? What did that mean? Sabine stared at her uncle. He sounded so unfamiliar, so Stasi-like.

"You have no idea who my friends are." Erich obviously wasn't admitting anything...yet.

"Let's see. How about Dietrich Spiller?" A little smile curled the man's lip, as if he held a winning hand of cards, and he knew it. "How about Greta Rathenau, or the Lueger twins? Oh, and Gerhard Fromm has proved quite helpful. Very informative."

He let the meaning behind his words sink in: *We know what you're doing. We know when you're doing it. And we know whom you're doing it with.*

It seemed Uncle Heinz had connections they hadn't even imagined. Much bigger than phone calls from the neighborhood spy.

"Oh, and by the way," he added, "even if they're released, your friends will stay on the state's watch list. But here's the good news: I'm not sure if you're on it—yet. That of course could change, depending on what you do now."

Erich didn't answer, so Uncle Heinz went on.

"Look, I'm trying to give you the break of a lifetime. In fact, I've even promised my friends that you won't make any more trouble. A second chance. Free and clear. What do you think of that?"

"I think you shouldn't have made that promise," Erich whispered back, never lowering his eyes.

"Why can't you understand this?" Uncle Heinz's cheeks turned flame-red. "The game you and your friends were planning, it's all over now. Done. Finished."

Erich silently crossed his arms.

"And because I keep my promises, here's my deal for you. You tell me you'll stay out of trouble from now on, and we'll forget we ever had this unpleasant conversation. Agreed?"

Incredible. Did Uncle Heinz really think Erich would agree to such an offer? Yet when he held out his pudgy hand to shake, Erich actually seemed to think about it. Finally he just shook his head and turned toward the door.

"I'll do my best, Onkel Heinz. But I really need to leave, or I'm going to be late for work."

"I can't help you if you run away, boy."

Erich left without another word. Sabine tried to follow.

"Wait a minute." Her uncle planted his foot in front of her right crutch. "The same goes for you, my girl. Whatever you've been doing lately ends here and now. *Verstehen Sie*?"

"Yes, I understand. But I have to go too, Onkel Heinz."

"You know it would kill your mother to find out you're mixed up in some kind of trouble, Sabine. I don't want to have to tell her, but I will."

A threat? Sabine pressed her lips together. Lifting her crutch over his foot, she hurried out the door.

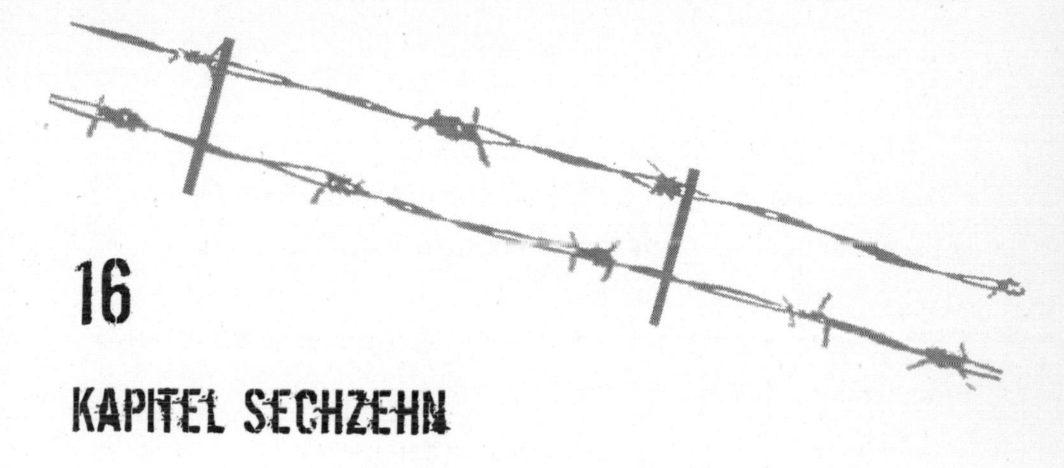

16

KAPITEL SECHZEHN

OUR FATHER

"The weird thing is, I think he really believes he's doing us a favor." Sabine stood in Willi's window the next morning, watching for American patrols on the other side of the wall. Anything to lift her spirits after yesterday's disaster.

Willi tinkered with his telescope, cleaning one of the lenses.

Sabine's mind raced as she looked down at the churchyard where they had planned to tunnel up to freedom. To *see* it from your window, but not have it? This was the worst torture of all.

"At least we don't have to schlep any more pails of dirt out of the tunnel." Count on Willi to try to make a joke. She punched him in the arm.

"That's not the point. The point is that—"

As she gazed at the churchyard, Sabine felt an idea start to bubble. She sometimes felt this way as she fell asleep, or in her dreams.

"I know how we can get out of here, Willi. Us *and* our families."

"And I still believe Snow White is a real princess." Willi rolled his eyes. "Come on. You said yourself the Tunnel Fellowship is dead. Your uncle made sure of that."

"No, really. I have an idea."

"Ja, ja. Your ideas always get us into trouble. What is it this time? Dig the tunnel ourselves?"

"Exactly."

Willi stopped chuckling at his joke. His mouth fell open when he realized she was serious. "I was just kidding, okay? We can't do it." He frowned. "Can we?"

She shrugged.

"You're saying this," he prodded, "even after the way you melted down the other day?"

She took a deep breath. Yes. Even after that.

"Well, let's think for just a minute," she said. "The tunnel still has about three meters to go, right? Ten feet?"

"I don't know. Could be a little more, could be a little less. I'm not sure. I'd have to measure it again. Neither of us has gone down there for a couple of days."

"But you know it's close, so we wouldn't have that much farther to dig, right?"

"I don't understand why you're trying to talk me into this. Sabine, the tunnel made you bawl. Don't you remember?"

She nodded quietly. "I remember. But what choice do we have?"

"Well, we could just forget the whole thing."

"After everything we've seen?" she demanded.

"I don't know, I—"

"After we saw that man get shot trying to escape?"

"You saw him. I heard him."

"After the Vopos stopped you for passing out our protest flyers?"

"Well—"

"After the wall went up in the middle of our city?"

He didn't answer.

"Besides, if we don't finish it now, someone will discover it. All that work will go to waste. It's not going to stay a secret forever, especially not with all the others in the fellowship being arrested."

"I hadn't thought about that."

"And so far, Onkel Heinz doesn't know we've been helping with the tunnel. He just thinks we've been hanging around the wrong people."

"Maybe we have."

"I'll pretend you didn't say that. Listen, Willi, we're the only ones who can finish this. Not even my brother can help now. They're watching him everywhere he goes."

Willi took off his glasses and rubbed his eyes.

"Do you know how they planned to come up exactly in the right place?" he asked.

"Not really. But you're smart. I know you'll figure it out."

Willi sighed. He couldn't argue with that, could he? He watched her. She sure knew how to put on a good face.

Most of the time.

But she couldn't keep the brave face on a few minutes later, when the telephone rang.

"Sabine? It's your mother," Willi's father said as he held the receiver out with a puzzled expression. She took it, knowing that her mother would not have called unless something was very wrong.

"It's your grandmother, Sabine." The voice on the other end of the line hardly sounded like her mother. "You need to come home right away."

Sabine closed her eyes and held on to her mother's hand as they sat in the first row of pews. Sabine had never attended a funeral in the big *Zionskirche* before. They'd sung a slow, solemn hymn. Then she'd watched the Reverend Karl Philip Speer ascend to the pulpit. He wasn't the regular pastor of the Zion Church. And surely he wasn't talking about their oma, was he?

Dedicated to our socialist ideals?

Someone who stood in the face of the capitalist West?

An example to the East German community?

Oh, she was an example, all right. But not the kind you're talking about, Sabine thought. *Who wrote this sermon—Onkel Heinz?*

At least he had shown up. Well, he'd lived in Oma's apartment for years, hadn't he? Aunt Gertrud sat next to him, stiff, bored, and with totally dry eyes. She checked her wristwatch more than once. And Sabine guessed she was probably skipping for joy under her cool mask—Oma was finally dead. She'd most likely start moving into Oma's bedroom as soon as they got home.

Sabine rested her head on her mother's shoulder, and she could not stop the tears from dropping like rain. She knew without a doubt that Oma was with Jesus—though the pastor hadn't yet mentioned their Savior's name. Oma Poldi loved and lived her life for Jesus. Sabine smiled through her tears at a memory of her grandmother praying with her when she was a child. She'd just come home from the hospital. It seemed as if she could still feel the older woman folding her wrinkled hands over Sabine's skinny ones, praying, *"Vater unser im Himmel—"*

"Our Father, which art in heaven—"

But that seemed so long ago. Now Sabine and her mother recited the prayer through their tears—and the memories would not stop: the little extra sweets Oma saved for her, just because. The laughs and the cookies, Berliner pretzels and *Mandelschnitten*—when they could find a few precious almonds. The way Oma slyly threw away socialist newspapers and then acted surprised, as if she couldn't find them! And how she opened her worn Bible and read to Sabine. She especially loved the stories of David and his friend Jonathan, or of Ruth—the faithful woman who stayed with her mother-in-law, Naomi. And of course the stories of Jesus.

If only this pastor would tell some of those stories. Oma would have liked that.

"*—vergib uns unsere Schuld—*"

"—forgive us our trespasses—"

Trespasses? Sabine couldn't help wondering why Oma had gotten so upset the last time they'd spoken in the hospital. What had this sweet, stubborn saint done to make her plead so for forgiveness? Sabine might never know. The secret had likely died with her in the hospital.

Listening again to the pastor, Sabine could tell he didn't know the real Oma. She was certainly not a Communist hero—

"*—wie auch wir vergeben unsern Schuldigem.*"

"— as we forgive those who trespass against us."

Sabine knew her mother believed as strongly as Oma. She'd often talked about growing up and how her mother, Sabine's other grandmother who had died years earlier, had shared her love of Jesus. Without moving her head, Sabine tried to glance at her uncle, just to see if he knew all the words. How could he not? Though he had rejected his mother and sister's God and replaced him with this country's un-god, had he really forgotten everything his mother must have taught him?

No—there! She saw his lips move, just barely.

"*Erlöse uns—*"

"Deliver us—"

Sabine peeked up at her mother. She knew that things had changed forever for her. The main reason she and her family had stayed behind in this bleak prison-city now lay in the simple wooden casket before them. And this modern-day Ruth and Naomi story would have a different ending from the one in the Bible.

In the Bible's version, Ruth stayed with her mother-in-law, Naomi, even after Ruth's husband, Naomi's son, had died. "Your people shall be my people, and your God my God." In the end, a nice rich guy named Boaz fell for the young widow, they got married, and everybody lived together happily. Sabine liked the story.

In their real-life story, the widow (her mama) remained as loyal to her mother-in-law (Oma). Maybe more. But Sabine wondered what had happened to the happy ending. Now she knew that their lives could change in just a few days, in a big way. And though she couldn't tell her mama about it yet, pretty soon she would have to.

Very soon.

But what about Willi's parents, sitting just one row behind her? How could she and Willi convince them to crawl through a tiny tunnel under Bernauerstrasse and escape to freedom through a graveyard? They'd have to leave their jobs behind. Their home. For what? Freedom? She shook her head. What was she thinking?

Uncle Heinz caught her eye, and his mouth snapped shut. Well, he could pretend not to pray, if he wanted to. She waited for him to nod, or wink encouragement at her, or shed a tear, or do something a person might do at a funeral. But he only held her gaze for a moment longer before turning away and whispering something to Aunt Gertrud. And for the first time,

Sabine hurt for her uncle, for what he had become, and for whom he had chosen to follow.

Because when Sabine looked up at the altar of the church, she did not see a figurine of Comrade Ulbricht hanging on that cross.

"*—in Ewigkeit, amen.*"

"—forever and ever, amen."

17

KAPITEL SIEBZEHN

BURIED ALIVE

"I don't know how Anton and Albricht dug so far." Sabine squinted as she hacked out a shovelful of dirt and let it fall behind her. She balanced awkwardly on a box as she reached up, praying she wouldn't come face-to-face with a coffin.

At least no one had talked about the tunnel. Not yet. If they did, Sabine and Willi would find out in a hurry.

"Just another couple of feet." Willi's voice sounded muffled. "We should be near the top."

After three days of digging, she sure hoped so. Sabine wiped the sweat from her forehead and tried to breathe. But her head spun and her stomach tumbled, almost as if she'd been playing on a playground carousel too long. When she closed her eyes, she saw stars around the edge of her vision instead of their flickering candlelight. And she knew if she didn't open her eyes soon, she would pass out.

But how long could it take to carve out ten feet of tunnel? At least this part arched nearly straight up, and they didn't need to keep plugging in wooden braces to keep it from caving in.

Sabine tried not to think of the dirt that covered her face. That got in her mouth and nose and eyes. That matted her hair. She didn't know if she could keep moving her arms, but she'd long ago stopped crying about it. And she tried to ignore the blisters that covered her hands. It seemed like the ground had changed a bit. More rocks and roots that made it hard to dig.

Never mind all that. She pushed again with the shovel, muscled past a couple of rocks, and widened the tunnel enough for her shoulders plus a couple of inches on each side. No telling who might use this escape, certainly not Uncle Heinz. She wondered what he would think, though, if he ever found out. Maybe he had already and was just waiting for them to come home so he could have them arrested.

"Well, that would be interesting, wouldn't it?" she asked herself. She could see how coal miners go crazy underground.

"What did you say?" Willi must have crawled in just below her to gather another bucketful of dirt.

"Nothing." She shook her head. "Tunnel diggers always talk to themselves, you know. Keeps them from—"

She didn't finish her sentence as she heard movement above her and tried to duck. No! She felt herself fall into a blender of dirt and rocks and roots. She didn't even have time to scream or to breathe. The tunnel just roared around her like a hurricane, twisting her head and sending her down.

At first it sounded like a dream. Like a ghostly *"Say-Beeeee-nuhhhh!"* over and over again. Sabine decided she must be dreaming, because she couldn't move her arms or legs. An awful, familiar feeling. Like waking up in the hospital all those years ago . . . in the starched bed that Nurse Ilse tied her to. In the dark closet that Nurse Ilse locked her in.

This dream had haunted her for years. But she knew that she could trade the dream for a better one. She could fly over the Swiss Alps, over the snow and the meadows, and the reddish-brown cows below would look up at her and moo.

"Please help me get her out of here, Lord!"

But the cows in her dreams had never prayed before. How odd. Someone grabbed her shoulders and bellowed into her face.

"You've got to breathe!" Actually, the voice sounded less like a prayer and more like pleading. "Wake up, Sabine!"

Just when she'd begun gliding over the nice, white snow?

But the shaking would not stop. Sabine blinked through a dirty crust to open her eyes. How unpleasant. Then she began to focus: Willi Stumpff, upside down, tears making tracks down his dirty cheeks, staring straight into her face—a lot closer than she would have liked. She tried to back away but couldn't move her head. And which side was up, really?

"You're alive!" He still sounded slightly like a cow.

"Haven't I always been?" She coughed and tried to wiggle her shoulders, then her arms. She blew through her mouth like a horse and tried not to spit dirt in Willi's face. As some of the dirt loosened, she rolled a little. And ouch, her shoulder felt like a pretzel.

"You must have loosened something up there," Willi told her. "Are you broken? I mean, is anything broken?"

"Twisted." She took stock of her body. "But I don't think broken." So Willi helped wrestle her out of the dirtslide. When she finally crawled free, something seemed different about the tunnel. They both looked up to find a sliver of light from a smallish hole.

"I meant to do that," she said with a smile. In her excitement, she didn't even notice all the dirt she'd swallowed. "Now we have to clear away this dirt and see where we came up."

But she stopped herself. First she had to tell him.

"I think you saved my life," she mumbled. "Thanks. But at first, I thought you were a cow in my dream."

"I thought I was supposed to be a sheep," he kidded, trying not to think about Sabine trapped in the dirt.

"You're not a sheep." She felt her voice catch, a tickle in her throat. "You... you dug me out, didn't you?"

"What else was I supposed to do?" he cracked, not allowing her to get mushy on him. "Now go see what's going on up there before somebody walks by."

Sabine could just imagine it: a pastor decides to take a walk near the graveyard, steps into the hole and—

"Come on, Sabine." Willi pushed her from behind. "Unless you really *did* break a bone."

If she had, she couldn't feel it now. She *could* feel a trickle of clean air coming through the opening, though, and she pointed her nose right at it. After breathing the damp, dead underground air for so long, it smelled delicious.

But she couldn't just poke her head up like a mole, could she? Willi pressed something into her hand.

"What's this?"

"You didn't think about it?"

She looked down at the small mirror. It looked like the one her mother used to put on makeup. Oh.

"Just hold the mirror up through the hole, and look around," he told her. "If we tunneled right, you should see the hedge. It should shield us so nobody can see us from the fence."

So while Willi waited, Sabine raised the mirror, like a submarine periscope. But instead of the hedge—

She pulled her hand right back down, as if she'd been burned.

"Can't be!" she whispered, and now she worried that someone might hear them. After all their work—

"What's wrong?"

"We're not where we thought we were." She looked like she might cry.

"Close?"

"Not close. We're in another part of the churchyard, too close to the wall. I don't know what will happen if we try to climb out right here."

"But if we don't?"

"But if we don't—and soon—someone's going to find the tunnel for sure."

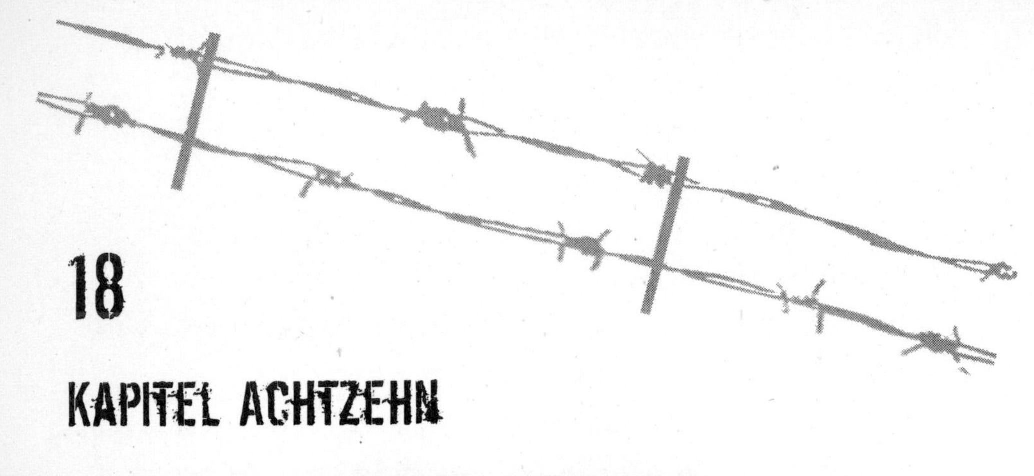

18

KAPITEL ACHTZEHN

LAST CHANCE

"Hold it, hold it, hold it." Sabine pulled up short. "We've got to think this through. We'll only get one chance to do it right."

Well, they always looked around before they left the ruins of the bombed-out apartment on Bergstrasse. Just to be sure. And that afternoon, she couldn't see any Vopos, but that really didn't mean anything.

"Right." Willi nodded. "So I'm thinking the only way we're going to convince my father is if both my mama and yours tell him they want to go."

"Maybe." Sabine tried to think through all the angles. "But I wonder if we should find a few more people and help them escape. After all that work Anton and Albricht did in the tunnel. We hardly did anything, compared."

"Yeah, but what are we supposed to do, march around the street with a sign: 'Freedom Tunnel: Open for Everybody'?"

"I just feel guilty, keeping it to ourselves."

She peeked out at the sidewalk once more, wondering. And even after changing into the clean set of clothes she'd stashed in the Volkswagen, she hoped she didn't actually look as if she'd just crawled out of a hole. Oh, well. Their first stop: St. Ludwig's.

"You did *what*?" Erich swiftly faked a smile and gave Sabine a hug when a dozen people in the hospital cafeteria turned to look.

"I said—," she started to explain.

"Little sisters," he said with his broad smile, but Sabine could almost see the steam coming out of his ears as he cut her off. "Always full of surprises."

He steered her to a quiet place in the hallway where he faced her and Willi. He looked like a parent who had caught the kids with their hands in the cookie jar.

"Tell me you're joking," he hissed, this time not so loud.

"It's done, Erich." Sabine crossed her arms and held her ground. She decided they had nothing to apologize for, no matter how mad her big brother sounded. "We finished it."

Erich's mouth hung open as he shook his head. "Do you have any idea how dangerous that was? You could have been buried alive! And who would have known?"

"*Ja,* Erich," Willi said. "You should have seen it. Sa—"

Sabine jabbed him in the side. They didn't need to tell that story just now.

"It's done, and we finished it, and that's all there is to it," she told her brother. "There's a little opening by the church."

Of course she didn't mention exactly how close to the church or to the wall, because Erich didn't give her a chance.

"An opening, already?" He rubbed his chin with worry. "That's not how we planned to do it. We were going to wait until—"

"We know, we know. It just, well, sort of happened that way."

No use telling the whole story about the cave-in. He already looked like he could have a heart attack any minute.

"Ja, but didn't you think someone could step right through it? Then we'd have Stasi swarming all over this side of the wall until they found the entrance. Did you even think of that? They're already breathing down our necks. One of the older nursing supervisors here watches everything I do. I think she helped get everybody arrested."

"Yes, we thought of it, Erich, and I don't need you to scold me. We just came for help."

Erich paced a little circle around them, but he didn't answer right away.

"And we wanted to ask you if we should tell anybody else in the fellowship," added Willi.

"Nein." Erich scratched his head and settled down a little bit. "I haven't talked to any of them since the Stasi swept through here. It's way too dangerous."

"So, what are you saying?" Sabine parked her hands on her hips. "That Willi and I did all that digging for nothing? Look at my hands! You want us to forget everything, because it's 'too dangerous'?"

That *wasn't* what they'd come to hear.

"Dangerous, yes. Forget everything, no."

"Excuse me?" Willi whispered out the side of his mouth, but Erich ignored him as he went on.

"Maybe you and Mutti should take this chance to escape. I think she'll leave now that Oma is...gone. She hates what this place is doing to you."

"Uh, you might want to look down the hall." Willi tried once more. "Is that the nurse you were talking about?"

The older woman had already started walking briskly toward them, clipboard in hand.

"You there!" the woman called as she approached. "A word with you, *bitte*."

"Go now," Erich commanded. "I'll take care of this."

"But—," Sabine objected.

"Go." He lowered his voice even more and checked his watch. "I'll meet you at home in an hour. Not a word to Onkel Heinz or Tante Gertrud. And be careful who sees you."

"What do you think she wanted?" Willi asked as he checked over his shoulder for the tenth time in the past block. Sabine didn't want to think about it. But she had a pretty good idea.

"You heard him. Everyone's being watched."

"*Ja*, but why didn't they arrest him, like everybody else?"

"I'll tell you why they didn't." She sighed. "My onkel. I think he's trying to use Erich to find the tunnel, so he can get all the credit. Maybe a pat on the back from Comrade Ulbricht."

"From the Goatee? How do you know that?"

"I don't, for sure. But I can't think of any other reason."

If she'd guessed right, though, the screws would tighten fast. They would have to make their move even sooner. So she kept up her pace for home. Bismarck loped along behind them as if he knew to stay close by. But she paused when they came to Willi's corner.

"You're coming," she told him, without looking up. "Nine o'clock at the Beetle. So we don't need to say good-bye. Okay?"

"Okay. But listen: you know my father might not... well, you know what I mean. So I want you to have something, just in case."

"Willi, I don't think—"

"Just wait here, all right?"

He disappeared into his apartment building before she could answer. In a couple of minutes, he returned with his telescope.

"Here." He held it out to her. "It's yours."

She wasn't sure how she would carry it. But what was she going to do, say no?

"Well, um, okay. Maybe just a loan. I'll borrow it until—"

Until what? They both knew that Willi might not come to the tunnel later. But Sabine wasn't ready to give up—not yet. She turned away, so Willi couldn't see her get blubbery, and hurried home. They didn't have much time.

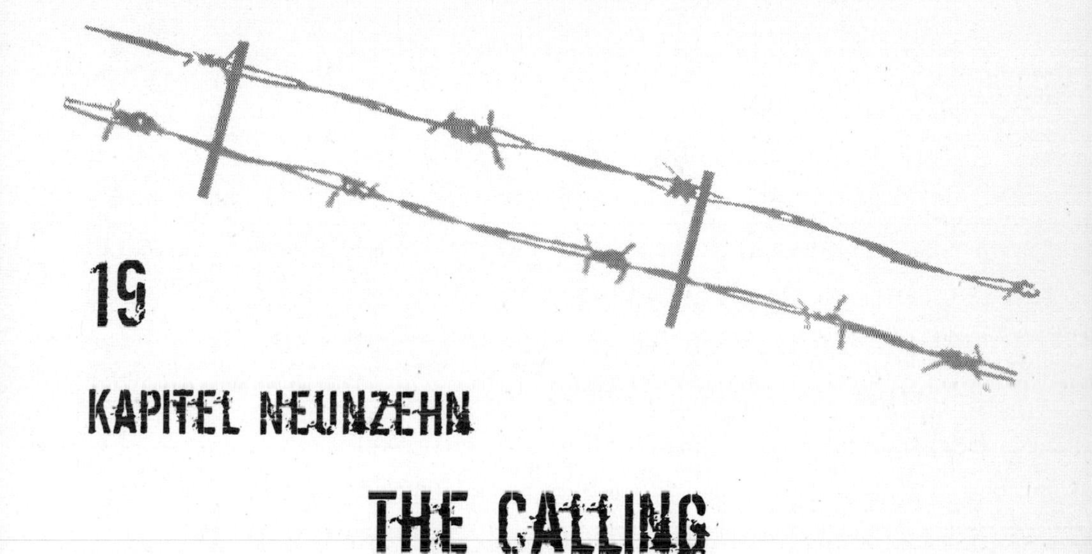

19

KAPITEL NEUNZEHN

THE CALLING

"You *have* to go, Mama." Erich could sound very convincing when he wanted to. "I promise, you'll never get another chance like this one."

"How can you promise that?" She sat in a kitchen chair with her arms crossed. "How can you know things won't open up again?"

"The wall?" He shook his head. "No, Mama. They're building it stronger every day. Adding more guards. More barbed wire. More no-man's-land. It's going to stay for a long, long time."

"Then why don't you come with us?" Sabine knew the answer before she asked it, but she hoped. And Erich looked at them with the saddest eyes she'd ever seen. Sad, but with a sparkle all the same.

"Remember how you always told us your place was here with Oma?" He leaned closer to his mother, his hand on her cheek. "You knew that God had called you here, for as long as Oma needed you."

She nodded as Sabine stood by, helpless.

"I guess I've always known God has called me to stay here, for the patients at the hospital." He turned to Sabine. "I haven't forgotten what you asked me in the alley, Sabine."

Neither had she. He didn't need to explain, but—

"When you asked if I still had a reason to stay in East Berlin. Well, I do. It hasn't changed. I'm staying."

Of course that only made their mother cry. Erich tried to dry the tears from her cheeks, tried to tell her not to cry.

"Mutti," he finally asked her, "don't you think this is what DeWitt would have wanted you to do for his daughter?"

Their mother gasped at the mention of Sabine's father, the American airman whose plane had crashed just weeks before Sabine's birth.

"He would have wanted me to do it a long time ago," she said as she reached out to take their hands. And with heart-wrenching sobs, she finally nodded.

"Good," Erich said. "But we'd better move quickly, or no one's going anywhere."

Sabine jumped when she heard the front door slam, the way it slammed when Uncle Heinz came in. Instantly they all straightened up and dried their tears.

"When's dinner?" he asked, poking his head into the kitchen. And his eyebrows rose when he saw them sitting together by the kitchen table. "Or are we just playing cards?"

Sabine's mother took a deep breath and stood up, though her brother had already returned to the other room.

"I need to tell you something," she announced. Erich shot up like a rocket.

"No, Mutti. Don't—"

But she held up her hand. She had decided, and there was no arguing.

"We're not just going to disappear without saying a proper good-bye," she told him, her chin set. "They're family, even if we don't always agree."

"We could write them a note," Erich suggested quietly. "A fond farewell, or—"

She shook her head firmly.

"We will tell them face-to-face, and that's all there is to it."

Sabine looked at her brother and felt like a leaking balloon, deflating slowly.

Mama has no idea what she's about to do—

An hour later, Sabine stood still in shock as she watched her mother and uncle hug.

"We're going to miss you," said Uncle Heinz. He rubbed his three chins and nodded as if he understood their decision.

Sabine couldn't believe what she heard. *Is this really Onkel Heinz?* His face looked almost like it had in the church, when he'd quietly recited the Lord's Prayer. Just for a moment. Good thing Aunt Gertrud had gone out that evening to visit her sister.

"And we'll certainly miss you too," replied Sabine's mother. She looked as if she meant it. Sabine had packed her toothbrush and a few small things, including Willi's telescope, in her backpack. They couldn't drag much with them through the tunnel.

"Don't get me wrong," her uncle replied, wagging his finger at them. "I don't like it, and I don't approve. And I'll probably regret this later, but—"

He stuffed his hands in his pockets and studied the floor. "But you're family, and I won't try to stop you."

Incredible. Sabine could hardly believe her ears.

Erich looked at his watch again and shifted on his toes. "It's dark," he announced. "We have to go now."

Sabine and her uncle nodded at each other; that was as close as she could come to a good-bye.

"We should wait for Gertrud," Frau Becker said as she looked out the window, hoping to see her sister-in-law. But Erich shook his head.

"We can't, Mutti. We only have thirty minutes. We have to go."

"I'll tell her you said good-bye," Uncle Heinz offered as he peered into the darkness over her shoulder.

"We'll write," promised Frau Becker. Of course, no one knew whether the letters would get through. Uncle Heinz nodded once more.

"I'll take care of everything. Even"—he hesitated—"even Wolfgang. Now go."

Sabine and her mother shouldered their bulging bags, as if they simply planned to go visit friends. And Sabine looked back at the kitchen once more, at the only home she could remember. Where would they live, over in the West? So near—only a few blocks away—but so far. Still Germany, but another country.

She waited impatiently to give her mother a head start. They couldn't walk together tonight. And she wondered as she watched Erich shake his uncle's meaty hand. Their sudden friendliness made her uneasy.

"I'm trusting you to come back tonight, nephew. And don't forget. You've got half an hour. After that, I guarantee nothing. If you're still there, you'll be arrested, just like anybody else. I won't be able to do a thing about it."

"Don't worry," Erich told him. "I'll come back. And you can take all the credit for finding the tunnel. That was our deal, and I'll stick to my end of it."

"See that you do."

Sabine gulped at their conversation. But it explained why Erich had watched the clock so closely. And now they had only twenty-nine minutes.

Ten of which they spent walking the long way around, down Bernauerstrasse and past the *bäckerei*. Then they doubled back behind the bombed-out apartment building. They'd all agreed that they couldn't look hurried, or worried, or anything of the sort. In her nervous excitement, Sabine fought the urge to look up and wave at the mysterious Wolfgang—the Watcher she wouldn't miss. But the last thing they needed was to have a Vopo stop and search them. She wondered if her bulging backpack might make Wolfgang suspicious anyway. The more she thought about it, the more she wished they hadn't packed any bags at all. Too late now. Erich and Sabine had reached the bombed-out apartment building and found their mother in the shadows. Quickly they showed her the trapdoor and helped her climb down. Sabine looked into the pitch-dark tunnel and sighed.

"I told them no later than nine." She looked out toward the street. "I thought for sure he would come."

Erich held the trapdoor open and shook his head.

"I'm sorry, Sabine. But—"

"I have to check." Maybe if she saw Willi and his family coming, she could hurry them up. "Just another minute. Give us one more minute."

"No, Sabine. There isn't time!" But Sabine had already started out, and Erich didn't want to drop the trapdoor, leaving their mother alone in the darkness below.

Sabine assumed he didn't follow her because he didn't want to risk making a scene on the street.

Unlike Willi, apparently—Sabine stared in surprise as she watched her friend stumble toward her, dragged along by—

"Bismarck! Come here, boy!"

Bismarck nearly bowled her down in his excitement as he showered her with sloppy dog kisses.

"Sorry we're late." Willi grinned all over. "We had a pretty long discussion, and—"

"You have no idea how late we are," she interrupted him. His parents followed at a short distance, just a couple with a new baby, out for a summer evening's walk. "What time is it, about nine-twenty?"

"I don't know. But the dog found me again, and—"

"Okay, okay. We've *got* to hurry. Get your parents to hurry up. The police will be here any minute."

"Go! Follow the tunnel, and don't look back," Erich whispered urgently as each person slipped through the trapdoor. He paused as Willi pulled the dog closer. "You can't take him."

"You know what he's like if we try to leave him up here," argued Willi.

Erich could only groan and shake his head. "Of course, he'll just whine and bring the Vopo right on top of us. Fine, take him. Just hurry!"

Last to go, Sabine stopped to hug her big brother one more time. She could hardly let him go.

"Change your mind," she whispered into his ear, burying her tears on his shoulder.

He held her close for another moment, then pushed her away.

"I'll see you again, little sister." His voice sounded teary too. She couldn't see his face clearly in the darkness. But she could hear the wail of a siren getting louder and louder.

And then she felt Willi's hands tug her through the trapdoor. Together, they raced through the darkened tunnels she knew so well. She knew every wooden brace, every curve.

"Sabine, are you coming?" her mother called back. Sabine could see her candle flicker up ahead.

"Right behind you, Mama."

"Come on, you. Move it." Willi poked at her. How had he gotten behind her?

"Going as fast as I can. I'm disabled, remember?"

"No, I forgot that."

Sabine gasped for breath as she finally got to the end of the tunnel. When she reached toward the opening, strong hands reached down to help her out.

"Come!" a strange man's voice insisted. "Follow the others, over there by the church." Willi popped up behind her, and the stranger hauled him out of the hole.

"Thank you," Willi said, breathing heavily. "Let's go. I'm the last one."

And a good thing too. They had hardly taken a step when headlights from the other side of the fence lit up the churchyard. Sabine stumbled, momentarily blinded by the light.

"Run!" she told Willi. "Leave me."

But he pushed her crutch out of the way and circled her waist with an arm. Off they ran, a three-legged race. They heard three pops, three shots, and Sabine knew the next one would be aimed straight at them—such a slow-moving target.

But they'd made it to the right side of the fence, right? Maybe that didn't matter. Bismarck had scrambled out of the hole and nipped at their heels. Sabine's mother ran back to help Willi and her daughter. But Sabine had to see, she had to know what happened. She looked over her shoulder and stumbled again.

"Sabine!" her mother cried as many hands grabbed at them, pulling them behind the protection of a large gravestone. But still Sabine had to see. She leaned out beyond the headstone.

Erich stood in the stark headlight glare, alone where God had called him to stay, surrounded by a swarm of Vopos leveling machine guns at him. What could he do but raise his arms in surrender? Sabine leaned closer, as if that would take her to her brother. But her mother held her back.

Jesus! she prayed silently. *Please keep him safe!*

They could only watch in fear from their little foothold in freedom. A policeman grabbed Erich from behind and forced him to his knees. Yet Erich held up his free hand and waved at his family.

"Oh, Erich." Sabine couldn't turn away as the Vopos dragged him off.

And then she stood with her friends and mother on the free side of the wall, and they hugged one another in a tearful celebration. One that had cost them too much.

"Welcome to West Berlin," the stranger who had helped them said. Sabine noticed for the first time that he wore a police uniform. As he led them away from the chaos of the wall, he added, "Congratulations. You're free now."

EPILOGUE

This story is dedicated to the memory of the 171 people who lost their lives seeking freedom from East Berlin. That's how many people were killed between 1961—when the wall went up—and 1989—when the wall came back down again. Those twenty-eight years were some of the bleakest in German history.

One of the bright spots came when an American president, John F. Kennedy, visited a divided Berlin in June 1963. He told a crowd of thousands in front of the Berlin City Hall that "when one man is enslaved, all are not free... [so] all free men, wherever they may live, are citizens of Berlin. And therefore, as a free man, I take pride in the words *'Ich bin ein Berliner.'*"

I am a Berliner.

But despite the speeches, the wall remained for many years. And just as in our story, people tried to escape from East to West in all kinds of ways. In the beginning, before the fence became a wall, they ran across or swam across one of the rivers or canals that ran through Berlin. They jumped from buildings that looked over the line. Some made it; some didn't. Some even escaped through the sewer system and dug tunnels. In fact, one of the first tunnels actually came up through a graveyard, until a woman accidentally discovered it by falling into the hole! And one of the most successful tunnels began in a basement near the line, just like in our story. Twenty-nine people made it to freedom through that tunnel.

One of the most interesting escapes came when two families—the Wetzels and the Strelzyks—secretly built a hot-air balloon and floated to freedom.

What does this tell us? That people will do just about anything to be free. And that sometimes, out of love, people will give their all so others can have that freedom. Dietrich Mendt, an East German pastor, used to quote Psalm 18 to explain why some East German Christians stayed behind the Iron Curtain, serving their neighbors and friends. "With God," the psalmist wrote, "one is able to leap over walls!"

These Christians didn't think the psalm told them to just jump over the wall, though. To them, it was a little more simple. They would stay and serve, and they would work for freedom.

Because for God, there really *are* no walls.

zonderkidz.

We want to hear from you. Please send your comments
about this book to us in care of zreview@zondervan.com. Thank you.

Grand Rapids, MI 49530
www.zonderkidz.com

ZONDERVAN.COM/
AUTHORTRACKER

CPSIA information can be obtained at www.ICGtesting.com
Printed in the USA
LVOW06s0259031014

407102LV00003B/10/P